SANTA
MONTEFIORE

SIMON SEBAG
MONTEFIORE

THE ROYAL RABBITS

RABBITS

OF

LONDON

ESCAPE FROM THE TOWER

Illustrated by KATE HINDLEY

This paperback editon published 2018

First published in Great Britain in 2017 by Simon and Schuster UK Ltd
A CBS COMPANY

1 3 5 7 9 10 8 6 4 2

Simon & Schuster UK Ltd
1st Floor, 222 Gray's Inn Road
London
WC1X 8HB

www.simonandschuster.co.uk
www.simonandschuster.com.au
www.simonandschuster.co.in

Simon & Schuster Australia, Sydney
Simon & Schuster India, New Delhi

A CIP catalogue record for this book is available from the British Library.

PB ISBN 978-1-4711-5791-2
eBook ISBN 978-1-4711-5790-5

This book is a work of fiction. Names, characters, places and incidents are either
the product of the author's imagination or are used fictitiously. Any resemblance
to actual people living or dead, events or locales is entirely coincidental.

Printed and bound by CPI Group (UK) Ltd, Croydon, CR0 4YY

Simon & Schuster UK Ltd are committed to sourcing paper that is made from
wood grown in sustainable forests and supports the Forest Stewardship Council,
the leading international forest certification organisation. Our books displaying
the FSC logo are printed on FSC certified paper.

To our darling daughter, Lily

SHYLO'S WARREN...

GABBAGES

THE FARMHOUSE...

HORATIO'S BURROW...

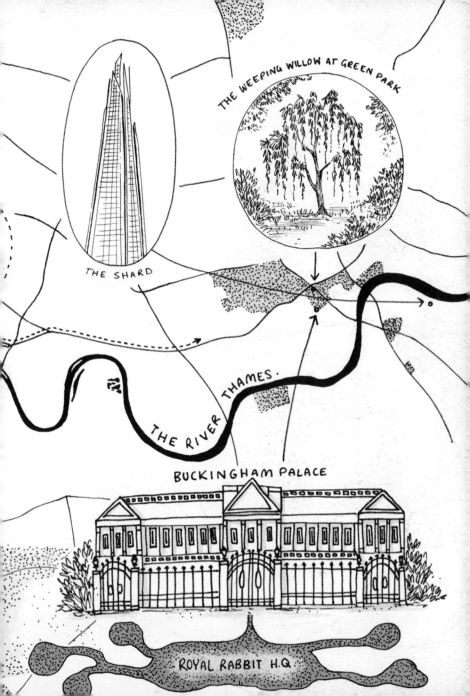

THE WEEPING WILLOW AT GREEN PARK

THE SHARD

THE RIVER THAMES.

BUCKINGHAM PALACE

ROYAL RABBIT H.Q.

THE RABBIT KINGDOM

buck male rabbit

bunkin country rabbit

bunny young rabbit

doe female rabbit

Hopster large, strong and clever rabbit

Jack Rabbit American rabbit

Thumper Special Forces
commando rabbit

CHAPTER ONE

It was six weeks since Shylo Tawny-Tail had left the small country farm he called home and set off on his mission to find the Royal Rabbits of London; six *long* weeks. Two rabbits in the countryside were missing him terribly. By some stroke of luck, they were about to find each other . . .

Horatio, the old, wise rabbit, was sitting in his shabby armchair, reading a newspaper he had 'borrowed' from the dustbin outside Farmer Ploughman's cottage. His burrow was warm because it was summer and the

scent of sweet grass and pine wafted down the tunnel from the forest above. But Horatio was lonely.

At times like these, he thought of Shylo. The small bunny used to visit Horatio to hear stories from Rabbit folklore. Here, in this burrow, Shylo had enjoyed learning about the Great Rabbit Empire of the past and the secret order of Royal Rabbits who still lived under Buckingham Palace and protected the Royal Family, and Horatio had loved teaching him. Then came the discovery of a plot to harm the Queen by a gang of super-rats called Ratzis, and Horatio had sent Shylo to London. His mission? To warn those Royal Rabbits and help them foil the plot.

Horatio had long suspected that, although Shylo was a weak and feeble bunkin with a squint, he had a brave heart. And the small bunny had become a hero just as Horatio had known he would.

The old buck sighed and tried to concentrate on the

newspaper, but, without the prospect of a visit from Shylo, he felt heavy of heart and strangely restless.

Just then, Horatio heard the light scamper of hesitant paws coming down the tunnel towards his burrow. He lowered his paper and narrowed his eyes.

'Who twitches there?' Horatio growled, rose from his chair and put his paw on his walking stick drawing out the secret sword that was hidden inside it. Horatio had once been a Royal Rabbit, and had only just escaped the Pack of snarling corgis - losing half an ear and earning many scars in the process. Now, on this quiet farm a long way from London, he was always ready and vigilant.

He sniffed the air. It didn't smell of dog but rabbit.

The scampering grew louder and then stopped in the mouth of Horatio's burrow. There came a soft thumping noise, for rabbits thump their hind paw politely when they arrive somewhere. 'Excuse me,'

murred a gentle, female voice. 'I'm looking for Horatio.' Then a small, anxious brown doe hopped into the light.

Horatio slid the blade back into his walking stick and looked at her curiously. She had big tawny eyes, a long, elegant nose and large ears. Horatio had seen those ears before. 'You must be Shylo's mother,' he said.

As the doe took in Horatio, her big tawny eyes grew bigger still. He was an enormous buck, quite different from the country rabbits she was used to. One of his ears looked as if it had been bitten off, he was missing one hind paw and his front left paw was wrapped in a bandage. The leaders of the Warren said that Horatio was mad and dangerous, and Mrs Tawny-Tail could see why they were afraid of him, but *she* wasn't. If he was a friend of Shylo's, she knew she had no reason to fear him.

'Please, take a seat,' he said returning to his chair, his voice no longer a growl but a soft murr. 'I now know where Shylo gets his bravery from. It is a very brave rabbit who ventures to my side of the forest.' He grinned and his eyes twinkled behind his glasses.

Mrs Tawny-Tail felt a little less frightened. She lolloped across the floor to the armchair opposite Horatio's and sat down.

'Shylo is not very brave,' she said and smiled tenderly at the thought of her clumsy, awkward bunny. 'I believed he'd been eaten by rats, but then I received a short note from him and this.' She put her paw in the pocket of her cardigan and pulled out a medal. The gold disc shone richly in the lamplight and Horatio could see clearly the special symbol of the Royal Rabbits - a crown with a pair of rabbit ears sticking out of the middle. 'I discovered Shylo's diary hidden beneath the mattress. That's how I found you.'

She glanced at the old buck shyly. 'It seems my son is especially fond of *you.*'

Horatio reached out and took the medal. He studied it closely.

'I was hoping you would tell me what it means,' she added.

Horatio removed his glasses. He looked at Mrs Tawny-Tail and saw the hope in her big, sad eyes. 'My dear Mrs Tawny-Tail,' he murred kindly, 'this is the Order of the Royal Rabbits of London.'

Mrs Tawny-Tail gasped. She had heard of the legendary Royal Rabbits, but hadn't believed they existed any more. 'But how is that possible?'

'Because Shylo is a brave and clever bunny,' Horatio murred. 'I sent him to London to warn the Royal Rabbits of a plot to harm the Queen and he succeeded where many would have failed. Not only did he help foil the plot, but he was also invited to join their

secret order. You have reason to be very proud of your son,' he said.

'My Shylo? A Royal Rabbit?' she repeated in amazement.

'Indeed.' Horatio handed back the medal. His face grew serious. 'But you must keep this knowledge secret,' he warned.

Mrs Tawny-Tail nodded. 'I'll tell no one.' She gazed at the medal and Horatio could see the pride gleaming in her eyes. 'Shylo loved coming here and listening to stories of the Great Rabbit Empire,' she murred softly. 'He's always been curious about the world. While my other children like to rag about, playing games, Shylo just wanted to read and learn.' Her gaze strayed to the bookshelves. 'No wonder he liked to come here.'

'Shylo has been a rewarding pupil,' Horatio mused.

'I wonder, would it trouble you to tell me a little about the Great Rabbit Empire and the Royal Rabbits of London? That would help me understand what Shylo is doing in London, and,' she murred in a shy voice, 'help me feel close to him.'

'It would be a pleasure,' said Horatio, pushing himself up from his chair with energy he had not felt since Shylo had last come to visit. He hobbled to the bookshelf and took down a large book. 'It's all in here,' he said, his nose twitching with satisfaction at the smell of old paper and leather. 'I'll share it with you, just like I shared it with Shylo.'

He sat and opened the book on his knee, then he smiled at Mrs Tawny-Tail, a smile that held within it the joy of reading, the love of history and the delight at having company at last.

'Life is an adventure,' he said, opening the first page. 'Anything in the world is possible - by will and by luck, a moist carrot, a wet nose and a slice of mad courage! Let us begin.'

CHAPTER TWO

High up in the very tallest point of London's famous skyscraper named the Shard, the Ratzis gathered. There were hundreds of them. A glistening seethe of rounded shiny backs, pink tails, black claws and yellow fangs, and the smell was horrendous: mouldy hamburgers, sour cream, rotten eggs and the stinkiest of farts.

You may think the top of the Shard is a very grand place for rats to have their offices. After all, the skyscraper rises high above all the other buildings like a gleaming glass dagger stabbing into the London sky. Indeed, it is so sharp and so tall that it should be called a sky*stabber,* not a sky*scraper!* And you'd be right: it is *much* too special for ordinary rats. But Ratzis are not ordinary. They are cleverer and more cunning and, instead of wriggling through garbage and sewers like normal rats, they root through the internet to weave webs of lies and hate. You could say they are digital rodents.

The office where they now gathered was white and glass and marble and had a magnificent view of London. They could see the dome of St Paul's, the clock face of Big Ben, the perfect circle of the London Eye and the stands of Wembley Stadium. And yes, somewhere in the haze they could see Buckingham Palace. In the floors below their lair were the luxurious offices of the mega media corporation, BubbleNet, which was also owned by the internet kingpin, Papa

Ratzi. As the people went about their business in the city below, they had no idea that above them lived a menacing colony of super-rats, plotting to wreak chaos on their world.

Now the Ratzis sat watching the giant screens which were playing all the channels Papa owned. They waited. Cameras with long telescopic lenses were slung over their shoulders, earpieces were clipped on to their ears and each one of them had the very latest smartphone or tablet; it was the Ratzis' job to record images and facts to feed the internet's endless hunger for the hearts and souls of people. Some famous, some not famous and some the most famous of all: the Royal Family. Every time the Ratzis succeeded in stealing something private, they stole a little of that person's soul and in so doing boosted their own power. You see Ratzis were greedy for happiness - *other people's* happiness. The more misery they created in the world, the more powerful they felt and the happier Papa Ratzi was with them (Papa's happiness was the only happiness they would accept).

The Ratzis tried to look respectable as they waited nervously to hear the orders of their mighty and frightening master, but looking respectable was an impossible task for a Ratzi. They scratched and farted and ground their jutting jaws that were powerful enough to crunch the hardest bone to powder.

None of them had ever even seen Papa Ratzi. He was a terrifying mystery. Some imagined him to be a grizzled old rat with prickly fur, others a ruthless young kingpin. Either way, he ruled an empire that controlled smartphones and search engines, satellites and screens, all over the world.

One thing they *did* know for sure was that he was brutal. If you were to look closer at the assembled rodents, you would see why. Each rat was missing

something. Some had lost one eye, the tip of their tail, the odd claw. Others had only half an ear. The very unfortunate had just three paws. None of them was complete.

The smallest, scraggiest and weakest-looking rat among them, dressed in a pristine white coat, was responsible for carrying out Papa Ratzi's terrifying 'tonic'. No one knew his name; they just called him 'the Doctor'. If Papa was displeased, the Doctor clipped off an ear or a paw . . . The rats were especially anxious today because a little country rabbit called Shylo had made a fool of them all.

For centuries, the Royal Rabbits of London had fought enemies and threats to the Royal Family and kept them safe. But then arose this twentieth-century empire of the internet, laptops and smartphones, and Papa Ratzi, with his army of super-digital mega-rats, had decided to use the new technology to defeat the Royal Rabbits once and for all. But, just at the moment of their first big attack on the Royal Family, Shylo arrived at The Grand Burrow and foiled their plan to embarrass the Queen. Plus three of Papa's best Ratzis had been eaten by corgis!

The Royal Rabbits' success had infuriated Papa Ratzi. You can call it Chance or Fate or Luck, but our unlikely hero, that squinting little rabbit, weak of stomach and floppy of ear, who had never even seen a smartphone and thought 4G was a sort of horse, had somehow saved the day.

Suddenly, a sickly-sweet tune broke the silence. It was the lullaby, 'Rock-a-bye Baby'. The scratching and farting stopped. The Ratzis shivered and looked around. Was Papa here? Or was he in Mumbai or LA? How would he appear to them?

Then vast words came into view on the wall, like a rolling hologram, as Papa started to type. There

was silence except for Papa's fingers on some faraway, invisible keyboard and a whispering as the Ratzis read his words aloud:

U call urselves Ratzis? Ratzis don't allow a little bunny from the countryside to outwit them. Ratzis don't allow a weak and feeble bunny to foil their plot and lead them to their deaths in the Kennel. I care about my Ratzis and would hate any of u to have to make an appointment with the Doctor...

A gasp rippled through the crowd as the Ratzis glanced at the rat in the white coat, whose secateurs glinted in his breast pocket.

Now u must prove to me that u are worthy of the name Ratzi. This is what I want u to do.

One of the fattest and greasiest Ratzis let off a loud fart. The other Ratzis stared at him in alarm. 'Oh, it just slipped out! Mercy, Papa!' cried Thigby, putting a trembling paw on the stump where one of his ears had been. The Doctor approached Thigby, twirling the secateurs in his claws, and Thigby shrank back, but then Papa began to type again.

Enough. No more interruptions. Now, I have news. The President of the United States of America is due to arrive for a State Visit in two days' time. He thinks he is the most important creature in the world. But who is really?

'You, Papa!' squeaked the seethe of rats.

I have plans for the President and no one, especially not Shylo, will stand in my way. I

want u to seize this Shylo and interrogate him. I want to know the Royal Rabbits' every secret and I want him out of the way so he doesn't scupper my plan.

The Ratzis quivered with excitement at the thought of seeking revenge on the rabbit who had humiliated them.

Mavis!

Slippery Mavis slunk forward. Out of all the Ratzis, she was possibly the ugliest, which is quite an achievement because Ratzis are, by nature, very ugly indeed. Her fur was a dull grey colour and balding in patches where she had scratched too much, and her belly was bloated from guzzling fizzy drinks. Her breath was so bad that she was known as the Fly-killer as flies that buzzed past her often dropped dead from a mere sniff of her breath. When Mavis smiled, she did so with only one side of her mouth, while the other side hung loosely over her jutting jaw from a fight she'd had with a badger. (The badger had lost.)

'I will catch this Shylo rabbit if it's the last thing I do,' she said. She plucked a flea, which had been happily snoozing, from her fur and popped it into her mouth.

U will not work alone.
Flintskin.

Now Flintskin stepped forward. His fur was black and moist, his nose and ears clammy and pink, but it was his two front teeth which set him apart from the other Ratzis. They were much too big for his mouth and stuck out like a pair of tusks. They could rip the skin

off even the toughest snake.

'I will not let you down, Papa,' said Flintskin and his eyes gleamed.

Of course u won't let me down. Because, if u do, I will send u to the Doctor. Phase two of the plan is as follows: my Ratzi army will embarrass the King and Queen and humiliate the President. I don't have to remind u that for the last hundred years a friendship has blossomed between America and England; after all, their people speak the same language. This Special Relationship is a powerful alliance that helps to keep peace in the world. But peace is our enemy. Bad news sells! So the more bad news there is, the richer and more powerful we become. U must find a way to ruin this Special Relationship. I'm counting on u.

Then the words disappeared. The Ratzis continued to stare at the space where they had been, too afraid to speak in case Papa was still listening. When the lullaby came no more, they began to murmur and mumble.

Mavis put out her pink tongue and licked her lips, dreaming of fame. Ratzis are greedy and cruel, but they also have a particular weakness: they want to be FAMOUS! To get a show on one of Papa's many TV channels; to have a million followers on Ratagram. If the Ratzis ruined the Special Relationship, they would become very famous indeed.

'We'll put Shylo in the Gym!' Mavis shrieked. Every rat in the Shard knew what 'the Gym' meant and they shuddered. For humans, a gym is a place of health and fitness, but for lazy, fat rats it is a place to be feared. Thus, the gleaming ranks of machines and weights in the Ratzi gym were instruments of torture.

'We'll put him on the running machine!' She rubbed her sticky paws together gleefully.

'Or the chest press,' said Flintskin. 'He'll never survive the chest press. That little bunny will wish he'd never left his burrow.'

Mavis laughed. 'Can't wait to see him on the rowing machine. That's broken even the toughest of our enemies. This should be a very easy job. That bunkin is no match for us.' She held up her claws and moved them in the light so that they glinted like knives. 'And, as Papa chose me first, once Shylo has spilled every secret, I will be the one to eat him.'

The other rats wriggled their bottoms together, doing the fearsome 'Driggle', jiggling their claws, rotating their bottoms and whirling their pink tails around their heads like lassos. If you ever see a Driggle - RUN! It's the war dance of the Ratzis.

CHAPTER THREE

Shylo was running so hard he could barely breathe. His heart was pounding against his ribcage and his blood was throbbing between his ears. The Ratzis were after him. They were close, *very* close. Close enough that he could smell their stinky breath and hear their shrill squeaking. He gasped for air and cried out. The little rabbit didn't dare look round. He wouldn't let them catch him. He *couldn't*. Not after everything he had achieved. Then he felt a claw scratching his back . . .

Shylo jumped and opened his eyes wide to see Belle de Paw, in her pink dressing gown, looking down at him. The beautiful amber-coloured doe was gently stroking his brow and soothing him with her French accent. 'Wake up, bunkin, you're having a horrible dream.' Slowly, Shylo realized where he was: safe in his bed in The Grand Burrow that lay right underneath Buckingham Palace. 'What was frightening you?' she asked.

'The Ratzis were chasing me,' he told her, his breath catching in his throat because, although the dream had gone, the terror hadn't.

'But they didn't catch you, did they?'

'No. I was running as fast as I could.'

'Nightmares are just your fears, Shylo. I dream about the Ratzis sneaking in to steal my jewellery.' She rubbed the diamond choker at her neck. 'Before you go to sleep, you must think of all the things you

love in the world.' She grinned and ran her paw down his damp cheek where tears had wet his fur. 'Celery?'

He smiled back shyly. 'Celery and my mother,' he murred.

'You see, if you think of those things, there will be no room for your fears. Don't forget that you defeated the Ratzis who were plotting against our beloved Queen.' She lifted his paw and showed him the special red sole that is the mark of a Royal Rabbit, reminding him of his adventure. 'You are one of us now,' she said. 'You are a brave and clever bunkin.'

'I think I was just lucky,' Shylo said modestly.

Belle de Paw shook her head. 'You made your own luck, Shylo, and you can make it again, as often as you wish. If you believe in yourself, there is no limit to what you can do. Now, think of celery and your mother and I will see you in the morning.'

Shylo was about to speak, but Belle de Paw bent

down and planted a kiss on his forehead, which silenced him because she was the most beautiful doe he had ever seen. 'Don't worry, bunkin, I'm not far away. If you cry out, I will be by your side in a second. We're a family here. We always take care of each other.'

Shylo watched Belle de Paw slip out of the door and close it softly behind her. He could still smell the sweet scent of her fur which was quite dizzying. He pulled the blanket up to his chin and closed his eyes. Even though he'd been here for several weeks now, he still wasn't used to sleeping in this bed; he didn't know if he would ever get used to being in the Royal Rabbits' Burrow.

But he did as Belle de Paw had suggested and thought of his mother. He wondered what she had made of the medal he'd sent her. Although she wouldn't know what it meant, she would at least be reassured that Shylo was alive and well. It had worried him greatly that she might think he was dead. Life in The Grand Burrow was so busy he didn't have time to think about the Warren he used to call home, but at night, when he lay alone in his bed, his mind was drawn back to the kitchen where his mother cooked at the stove, and he could almost smell the familiar scent of carrot pie and feel her soft face press against his as she bent down to give him a kiss.

He tried to be brave, after all, he was a Royal Rabbit now, but if he could have had a few minutes with his mother he would have whispered in her ear that he was really quite homesick sometimes. Shylo didn't, however, miss his siblings, least of all his older brother Maximilian, and he knew that, was he ever to go back, he would never allow them to bully him again.

This certainty gave him a warm sense of pride. He might have been a little lucky in foiling the plot to embarrass the Queen and he might not be quite as

brave as the Royal Rabbits thought he was, but he knew that he was now strong enough to stand up to Maximilian. Simply being a member of the elite band of Royal Rabbits had given him the confidence to do so.

Shylo thought of celery, he thought of the cosy Warren and he thought of his friend Horatio, and how proud he must be to know of Shylo's success. Slowly, he drifted off to sleep and in his dreams there were no Ratzis or corgis to terrorize him, only the roly-poly fields and soft green meadows of home.

CHAPTER FOUR

The following morning, Generalissimo Nelson, the leader of the Royal Rabbits, summoned Shylo to his war room for a meeting with Clooney, Belle de Paw, Laser and Zeno, his four most important Hopster rabbits. (Hopsters are not like ordinary rabbits you see munching on grass in London parks; no, these highly intelligent and vigorous rabbits are bigger, more muscular and very capable.)

The most dashing of the four was Clooney. His official title was Groom of the Tail (and he certainly

liked grooming himself), but really he was a secret agent. He was a very handsome rabbit - if a little vain (no one's perfect!) - with long grey ears and an intelligent expression on his charming face. He wore a black dinner jacket with smart black trousers, a scarlet bow tie and cummerbund.

As Shylo entered the room, Clooney was draped over the sofa in Nelson's war room, admiring himself in a silver mirror and grooming his grey fur with a tortoiseshell comb he kept in his breast pocket for that very purpose. (It's important to note that most of the time, when Clooney appeared to be gazing at himself in a mirror, he was actually spying on those behind him who didn't know they were being watched. You could say that his vanity was a good disguise for a very dandyish spy!)

Belle de Paw's official position was the Doe of the Dressing Table. Her job was to look after the security of the Queen's bedroom. Now she was at the periscopes in a sparkly blue dress with a feather boa, observing the coming and going of everyone in Buckingham Palace above, from the Royal Family to the maids and footmen and Special Protection Officers. Belle de Paw also used the periscopes to look for anything that glinted. What she liked doing best was 'borrowing' the odd diamond or ruby from the Queen's boudoir, which she was certain Her Majesty would not miss.

'When you have so many, what is one less?' she would say in her soft French accent, flashing her jewels.

Laser was an American rabbit and her job, besides being a secret agent, was linking the Royal Rabbits of London with the Rabbits of the White House. She was a very colourful, even garish, sight. The fur on her arms was dyed red, white and blue, stars and stripes, and she wore bright scarlet trousers with a blue stripe down each leg. She was all the colours of

33

the American flag! On her back she carried a bow and a bag of arrows, and tucked into a belt at her hips was a whip. Laser was feisty and energetic and always ready for action. Right now she was studying the map table with her sharp eyes narrowed.

The last, but by no means the least important, Hopster was the loud and muscly Marshal of the Thumpers, who was called Zeno. This big black buck was enormous and his voice was so loud that the chandelier in the great hall would sometimes tinkle when he spoke. Zeno commanded the army of Thumpers who were the Special Forces commando rabbits. He was very strong and brave, and everyone was a little afraid of him. They would be less afraid, however, if they knew his secret: that he was VERY frightened of thistles and elastic bands! (*Shhh,* please keep that information to yourselves . . .)

Every Royal Rabbit had taken an oath to protect

the Royal Family from harm, and had the sole of one paw painted red, called the Badge, as a mark of great distinction. Nelson, the Generalissimo, had *two* red paws, which was known as the Double Badge.

As Shylo hopped into the war room, Nelson looked at the little bunny over his spectacles. 'Ah, Shylo,' he gravelled. 'Now we can start.' The old grey buck hobbled to the map table, leaning on his baton with its silver rabbit head. 'Royal Rabbits, gather round,' he commanded in his deep voice.

Shylo gazed up at the heroic Hopsters collecting around that famous table. He was barely able to believe that he was here in The Grand Burrow, not as an Outsider but as a Royal Rabbit, a wearer of the Badge.

As Shylo took his place, Zeno patted him on the back: 'Hello, you little monster,' he said, his Jamaican accent coming through clearly as he used his affectionate

term for rabbits he liked. His pat almost knocked the life out of Shylo. The little bunkin hopped to the table to stand between Clooney and Laser. He lifted his chin and pulled back his shoulders, standing as tall as he could, but he still looked tiny compared to the towering Hopsters.

'POTUS is due to arrive in London in two days' time to visit the King and Queen,' said Nelson.

Shylo raised a paw shyly.

'What is it, Shylo?' said Nelson, peering over his spectacles.

'What is POTUS?' the little bunny asked.

'It means President of the United States,' Nelson replied.

'Ah,' said Shylo.

'ROTUS will arrive with their President on Air Force One, the President's plane,' Nelson continued. 'And ROTUS stands for?' he glanced at Shylo.

'Rabbits of the United States?' Shylo suggested timidly.

'Clever boy! You see, Shylo, America was once an English colony ruled by King George III and his Royal Rabbits. But the Americans rebelled and won their independence. The rabbits in America decided to stay and help the President run the new country, the United States. When the first President, George Washington, built the White House, he didn't even notice the rabbit tunnels running beneath it. Right under the Oval Office, where the President works, is the Oval Burrow. Just like here, the humans think they run things, but we all know that, without rabbits, nothing would ever get done. We'll make ROTUS welcome here and together we will ensure that the President's visit runs smoothly.'

The Generalissimo looked at Shylo and his old face turned very serious. Shylo was reminded of Horatio for

he had had the same expression when he had taught Shylo about the Ratzis. 'Britain and America have a very close friendship,' he continued. 'Nothing can be allowed to ruin this Special Relationship. It's part of the very foundation that helps us work together with other countries to keep the peace.'

'The Ratzis would love to spoil everything,' said Belle de Paw. 'If we are weaker, they are stronger.'

'We can deal with *them*,' said Laser, baring one gold tooth, and tapping her paw against the whip in her belt. 'We won't just talk the talk,' she said, 'we'll walk the walk.' And she did, strutting round the table in her leather boots.

Laser is just amazing, Shylo thought, watching her with admiration.

Just then there came three knocks on the door and the Major-domo, who was a short, round doe in a red-and-gold ceremonial uniform, whose duty it was to run The Grand Burrow, hopped in. 'Generalissimo,' announced Frisby. 'Rappaport has news. He awaits you in the Shack.'

Nelson rubbed his chin thoughtfully, then said, 'We will come at once.'

Shylo followed the big Hopster rabbits down into the very deepest tunnels of The Grand Burrow. They descended a spiral staircase, cut into the earth like a giant corkscrew. The air around them grew cooler and a little damp until at last they reached a dimly lit room where a blotchy and almost hairless rabbit was on his knees at the back of a massive, old-fashioned computer, fiddling about with wires. Suddenly, a spark flew out, just missing the rabbit's ear, then the computer jumped to life and began to whirr and rumble like a washing machine. Satisfied, the patchy rabbit stood up to greet the Generalissimo.

Rappaport was not at all like the other Hopster

rabbits. He was squat and flabby with a round belly and watery blue eyes, as pale as mist, which were almost completely hidden behind a pair of thick glasses. He twitched nervously, putting his paws in and out of the pockets of his rather food-stained pinstriped suit. He looked like he had lived underground all his life, Shylo thought.

'Ah, Rappaport,' gravelled Nelson. 'What news?'

'Danger: we have learned that the Ratzis had a Driggle last night. Always a bad sign.' Rappaport pointed at his screen where they could see the outline of the palace with red dots circling it. 'You see, Ratzis are now staking out the palace,' he said.

Nelson looked at those red dots and narrowed his eyes. 'Are they indeed?'

'They've never done that before,' said Laser.

Rappaport nodded. 'No, they have not. But the President's visit is the biggest chance they have ever

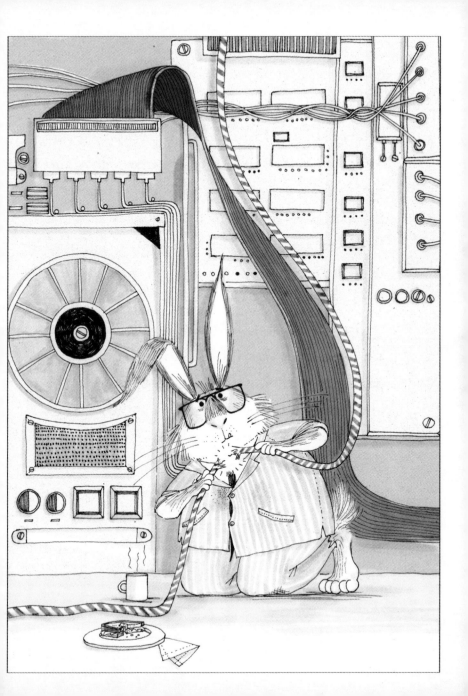

had to create a world crisis.'

'That is true,' growled Nelson.

'But they're chaotic. You can see from their movements that there's no orderly plan. I suspect this is just a patrol to see what they can find,' Rappaport suggested sensibly.

'I hope they find nothing,' said Belle de Paw, putting her paws on her hips.

'We must all be careful coming and going beneath the Weeping Willow.' The pale rabbit twitched his nose and shuffled on his hind paws. Suddenly, the computer groaned and went dead. Rappaport banged it hard with his fist. It flickered erratically before lurching back to life.

'Indeed,' murred Nelson. 'Clooney, you, Laser and Shylo go immediately to Number Ten and talk to ST-BT. See if he has more information.'

'Yes, sir,' said Laser, winking at Shylo.

'Yes, Generalissimo,' said Shylo, thrilled to be given an important task with Laser and Clooney.

'Understood,' murred Clooney, straightening his bow tie in the reflection of the computer screen.

'Good,' said Nelson, satisfied. 'Nothing must destroy the Special Relationship.'

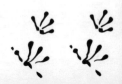

CHAPTER FIVE

'Come on, Shylo,' said Laser, setting off with Clooney by her side. 'It's time to introduce you to ST-BT.'

Shylo hurried behind the two Hopster rabbits, up the spiral staircase, across the great hall and through the round door to the tunnel where the cart which had brought Shylo to The Grand Burrow that first day now waited on the train tracks to carry them to Number Ten Downing Street, the Prime Minister's house.

'You may not realize this,' said Clooney to Shylo, 'but London is a city of tunnels. To use them you just need to know where they are.'

These tracks ran along the tunnel - like a small railway down a mine. The rabbits hopped into the cart that set off at once with a jerk and a screeching of wheels. As the wind swept through Shylo's fur, he wondered who ST-BT was. Maybe another rabbit, or perhaps a mouse or a hedgehog? But when he hopped out of the cart, which eventually came to a halt outside a pair of sliding doors, he smelled the unmistakable and alarming taint of fox.

Shylo froze. Foxes ate rabbits where Shylo came from. In fact, being eaten by a fox was possibly just as bad as being eaten by a corgi, Shylo thought.

'It's OK,' said Laser, sensing Shylo's panic. 'You have nothing to worry about. Those of us who protect the realm have a special code. The foxes here

won't eat you.'

Shylo gulped. He felt his courage flag. 'Easy, Shylo,' said Clooney gently. 'Didn't Horatio teach you the most important Rabbit Rule of Secret Craft? Trust. When you took the Oath of Allegiance, you agreed to trust us. Come along and stop trembling. ST-BT has no patience for wimps.'

Laser patted his thin shoulder. 'Come on, Shylo,' she said kindly, grinning down at him. 'I know just how brave you are.' He looked up at her and she winked. His flagging courage rallied a little.

The double doors slid open and Clooney and Laser hopped through them into a dark tunnel. Shylo had no option but to follow. The smell of fox was stronger now. It came in thick clouds, pungent and spicy. It wasn't unpleasant like Ratzi stench and corgi breath, but it put fear into Shylo's heart; many a rabbit in the Warren had been devoured by foxes.

Shylo followed the Hopster rabbits down the long tunnel. The dark didn't bother him for rabbits eat carrots so they can see in the dark, but the fox smell was getting stronger all the time and, in spite of Laser's reassurance, Shylo's heart began to beat very fast.

After a while, the tunnel started to climb steeply and the Hopster rabbits scampered up it until they reached a green baize hatch at the end. Clooney pushed it open. Shylo watched them jump into a large white room. He hesitated; here the taint of fox was almost overpowering, and he had to gather all his courage to follow them. But follow them he did, because Clooney was right: he trusted his friends; they wouldn't lead him into danger.

Shylo could hear the beat of rock 'n' roll music coming from behind a big white door with a shiny brass knob.

'We are now directly below the Prime Minister's

office at Number Ten Downing Street,' Clooney said to Shylo as he turned the brass knob and opened the door. 'Welcome to the Fox Club.'

Shylo hopped into the room.

His heart contracted with fear: red fur; red bushy tails; white teeth. FOXES EVERYWHERE.

Sleek, smartly dressed foxes sat on high velvet chairs at a gleaming zinc bar. Some drank colourful cocktails with straws and some sipped coffee from small espresso cups. Some leaned over a green felt pool table, wielding billiard cues, while others lounged around card tables, playing poker or spinning roulette wheels as if this was a casino. Others were dancing to the jukebox. A fox threw darts at a board, always hitting the bullseye. There was another group chatting in big leather chairs, talking in low voices. And everything in the Fox Club was shiny and glossy and bling.

Shylo's eye was drawn to an enormous oil painting hanging above the bar. It was of the coolest-looking fox of all, riding a Harley Davidson motorbike. His red-whiskered face was wide and good-looking, his fur rich and silky, his yellow eyes bright and shining with intelligence. On the gleaming oil tank of the Harley Davidson, in big gold letters, were the initials ST-BT.

At that moment, a pair of double doors swung open. The room fell silent and still. Only the music continued to play. There, standing in the door frame, a giant fox was silhouetted against the light that shone behind him. He had one arm raised and one paw off the ground in a flamboyant pose.

Shylo caught his breath.

His heart stopped.

The fox was so strong, so obviously powerful, that Shylo's ears drooped and he shrank behind Clooney and Laser with fear.

ST-BT strutted into the room. Of all the foxes in the world, he was, Shylo thought, surely the most debonair, the most lustrous, the most pearly-toothed fox that ever existed. His white-tipped red tail was luxuriant and extravagantly bushy. His face was wide, his nose haughty, his whiskers magnificent. He wore red trousers with a black stripe down each leg, polished black boots and a white leather jacket with shiny black buttons. On his wrists shone silver cufflinks engraved with his initials and on his paw flashed a big silver ring. A golden necklace of chunky letters spelling out STBT hung around his neck.

Shylo watched the fox walk into the room - no, it wasn't a walk, it was pure SWISH. The little rabbit tried to rouse his wilted ears so that ST-BT wouldn't sense his fear.

But ST-BT missed nothing.

His nose picked up even the slightest emotion and

he peered down at Shylo. 'And who is this nervous little creature?' he asked, his voice crisp and deep.

'This is our newest recruit,' Clooney told him, sliding on to one of the high chairs at the bar and asking the bar-fox for an espresso. Clooney, ever suave and handsome, spotted his own reflection in the espresso machine and, pretending to admire himself, he watched the foxes in the room behind him who were all blissfully unaware of his gaze.

'Does he speak?' ST-BT asked, narrowing his eyes and looking Shylo up and down.

'Of course he speaks,' said Laser, jumping to Shylo's defence. She gave Shylo a prod.

The small bunkin seemed to wake from his trance. 'My name is Shylo,' he murred in a small voice. He suddenly remembered to give the sign and raised his Red Badge.

'And my name is Sharp-Tooth-Bushy-Tail, but my

friends call me ST-BT.' The glossy fox chuckled and Shylo felt as if a cold wind had just swept over his fur. 'So, you're a member of the Royal Rabbits, are you? You don't look like one.'

'He's braver than all of us put together,' said Laser, which Shylo knew wasn't true, but he felt happy that Laser wanted to back him up.

'You're frightened of me, Shylo, I can smell it,' said the fox, putting his nose to the bunkin's face. 'But you're not from here, are you? You're a long way from your country home.' Shylo's eye widened (the other, remember, was concealed behind his red eyepatch). 'Don't look so surprised; it's my job to know everything.' He straightened and put his paws on his hips. 'I'm not going to eat you. I've eaten so many rabbits in my time that I've grown bored of the taste. It's not flesh I crave but power.'

'I'm most relieved to hear that, ST-BT,'

said Shylo meekly.

The fox grinned, flashing his sharp white teeth. He put out his paw and clicked his claws. Immediately, a fox in a black waistcoat and white shirt brought him a glass of Butterscotch on the Rocks. It matched ST-BT in its creamy richness. Shylo watched the fox put the straw to his lips and take a sip. The murmur of voices resumed once again as the foxes in the club went back to their gambling and their darts.

'Butterscotch on the Rocks, little rabbit? Or would you prefer a carrot juice?'

'A carrot juice would be very nice, thank you,' Shylo replied politely and

ST-BT clicked his claws once again and a carrot juice was swiftly delivered.

Noticing that Shylo was gazing around him with wide, curious eyes, ST-BT put a heavy paw on his shoulder. 'Come, let me show you around.' He sauntered over to a row of periscopes, much like the ones Shylo had already seen in The Grand Burrow. ST-BT pulled one down to Shylo's level. 'Take a look at Number Ten Downing Street,' he said. 'The heart of British power.'

Shylo expected a grand palace, but what he saw was a rather normal-looking house made of charcoal-coloured bricks with a black front door in a white frame. If it wasn't for the two police officers guarding it, he wouldn't have known it was important at all. He couldn't help feeling a little disappointed.

'Foxes have been helping the Prime Ministers of Great Britain ever since the first Prime Minister Walpole brought a fox cub into Downing Street as a present for his son. If it hadn't been for us, the Duke of Wellington would never have won the Battle of Waterloo, Gladstone and Disraeli would have ruined the Empire, and Churchill would have lost the Second World War!' ST-BT pointed to some chairs around a card table. 'Take a seat, my friends,' he said.

Laser and Clooney sat down and Shylo followed their example. But the little rabbit was so small he was only just able to see over the table in front of him. ST-BT settled himself into a leather armchair, facing Shylo, and licked the butterscotch off his top lip.

'I have thousands of foxes working for me in every corner of the city,' he said. 'The Backstreet Brushes live in people's gardens, roam the pavements, parks and playgrounds, peer into people's houses and sometimes even curl up on their sofas if they desire a comfortable night's sleep. There is nothing that goes

on in this city that I don't know about.' He turned to Clooney and Laser. 'So, what can I do for you?'

'As you know, the President is arriving in two days' time,' said Laser. 'The Ratzis pose a dangerous threat to the visit and we need to know their every move . . .'

'Yes, I have something for you. My Brushes have spotted a couple of Ratzis loitering dangerously close to the Weeping Willow in St James's Park. They had a net and a stick of celery. You must all be vigilant.'

Clooney looked alarmed. 'The Weeping Willow is the secret entrance to our Grand Burrow.'

'It doesn't sound good,' said Laser. 'We'll tell Zeno to double the guard on all the tunnels beneath the palace while the President is here.'

'We are living in dangerous times,' growled ST-BT. 'Life was simpler when we were dealing with the odd thief and spy. Papa Ratzi's rise to power and the dangers of the internet have given us something seriously worrying to think about.'

Shylo, who had so far said nothing, piped up in his small voice. 'Horatio always told me that everything in life has a good side and a bad side. The internet can be good if it's used by people who want to learn facts and chat to friends, but to those who want to spread lies and hate, like the Ratzis, it's a very dangerous thing indeed.'

ST-BT looked at Shylo as if he had said something so dazzlingly brilliant that the little bunkin felt himself grow hot with surprise and pleasure. 'Horatio?' ST-BT repeated with a frown. 'You know Horatio?'

'Yes, Horatio taught me everything I know,' Shylo replied. 'He sent me to find the Royal Rabbits when I overheard a Ratzi plot against the Queen. It's because of him that I'm here.'

ST-BT's expression softened. It seemed he had been rash to judge Shylo on his frail appearance. 'Anyone

who is a friend of Horatio's is a friend of mine,' he said. 'Horatio found me when I was a cub after my mother was killed by Pest Control. I'd curled up in a bin to keep warm and if it wasn't for him I would have surely died the following morning when they came to collect the rubbish.'

'Horatio is like a father to me,' said Shylo, whose own father had been shot by the farmer back home.

'He's like a father to me too,' said ST-BT with a wistful smile. 'I was so happy to hear from Nelson that he hadn't been killed in the Buckingham Palace Kennel, after all, but escaped the corgis and fled to the countryside.'

Laser glanced at Clooney; neither had ever met Nelson's brother. 'I'd sure like to know this Horatio,' said Laser. 'He sounds like a very cool guy.'

'He was the bravest of all the Royal Rabbits,' said ST-BT. Then he knitted his claws and looked directly at Shylo. 'What advice would he give about the President's visit, do you think, Shylo?'

Shylo thought for a moment. He knew his answer was important if he wanted to be accepted as a Royal Rabbit by this swishsome fox. 'I think Horatio would say: "Life is an adventure and anything in the world is possible - by will and by luck, a moist carrot, a wet nose and a slice of mad courage."'

ST-BT threw back his glossy head and gave a rumbling laugh. 'He would indeed,' he bellowed, slapping his thigh. And suddenly the whole Fox Club was laughing with him and Shylo, who was still slightly anxious about the sheer number of foxes in the room, found himself quietly laughing too.

CHAPTER SIX

Shylo returned to The Grand Burrow with Clooney and Laser. He was so relieved to be out of the swanky Fox Club, where the scent of fox had been almost unbearable, that he forgot that the Backstreet Brushes had spotted Ratzis lurking around the Weeping Willow and hurried outside for some air. Shylo always felt better being in nature and he looked about him and felt instantly comforted.

By now it was early afternoon. The summer sunshine flooded the park and a gentle breeze made a rustling sound in the branches above him. He breathed in what *should* have been the sweet grassy smell of the park, but instead was the revolting stench of rotting junk food and farts. He froze and glanced about him. There was no sign of rats, just the merry laughter of children as they played with a small dog some way off in the distance, and the gentle rumbling of traffic on the Mall.

However, Shylo's sharp sense of smell was never wrong. And above him, hidden in the leafy branches of the Weeping Willow, were Mavis and Flintskin.

'Stop farting!' Mavis hissed crossly. 'Can't you hold them in even for a minute? The rabbits will smell you.'

'They just slip out,' Flintskin complained.

'That's what Thigby said and it nearly cost him his other ear.'

'Hmm. True. No more seeping out then! But we've been waiting here for hours. I'm bored. And hungry.

You said you'd seen rabbits under here, but we haven't seen so much as a fluffy tail in . . . Wait! What's that?'

They both looked down to where Shylo was standing in the shade of the tree.

'That's him!' whispered Mavis. She leaned over to get a better look. 'Just like they described: small and feeble-looking with a red eyepatch. Of all the luck!'

'Shouldn't be difficult to catch,' said Flintskin.

'Can't imagine how a little runt like him could have got the better of Baz, Grimbo and Splodge. Idiots!' She poked Flintskin with her claw.

'Ouch!' he whined.

'What are you waiting for? Throw down the celery!'

'Oh right, yes, the celery.' Flintskin let the stick of celery drop to the ground. It landed with a thud right next to Shylo.

The little rabbit had been busy looking for Ratzis. He knew he smelled them. But he couldn't see any rats anywhere. The sudden noise jolted him from his search and he spun round to find a stick of celery lying on the grass beside him. At the sight of his favourite vegetable, Shylo's heart gave a leap and he forgot all about the smell of Ratzis as his one eye feasted on it with surprise. How deee-lish. How tempting!

Above him the two Ratzis were trembling with excitement. 'Now drop the net,' instructed Mavis.

Flintskin got ready to throw down a net that was just big enough to catch a small rabbit like Shylo. At this point, it seemed as if it was going to be much too easy for the Ratzis to trap the poor bunkin. But Mavis's mouth was watering so much at the sight of the rabbit that her drool overflowed her drooping lip and a large dollop dripped, in a green, greasy globule, right on to the piece of celery, just as Shylo was about to pick it up.

At the same moment that the globule landed, Laser

poked her head out of the hidden entrance to The Grand Burrow. 'Shylo, you're needed. Come quick!' she said.

'Drop the net!' screeched Mavis.

Flintskin threw down the net and for a second it hovered over Shylo's head. But in the nick of time Shylo dashed towards Laser and down the manhole into The Grand Burrow. So all the net caught was the soggy piece of celery.

'You idiot!' cried Mavis, pushing Flintskin off the branch so that he landed on the net with a squeal. He rolled and squirmed, but his flabby body acted as a cushion so he didn't hurt himself at all. Rats are very resilient. Ratzis even more so.

'Who are you calling an idiot?' Flintskin screeched back, baring his two sharp teeth. 'You dribbled on the celery!'

'*You* farted and he smelled it!'

'*You* were too busy thinking of your stomach!'

'*You* were too eager to be famous!'

Mavis swung down one of the long branches and landed beside him. 'You're going to have an appointment with the Doctor!'

Flintskin grinned grimly. 'Then so are you. We're in this together, don't forget. If I fail, *you* fail.'

Mavis scowled and her face became even uglier, which one would not have thought possible. But then her drooping lip slowly lifted into a smile as she rested her eyes on the bush into which the rabbits had disappeared. 'Wait . . . I think we've just stumbled upon the secret entrance to the Royal Rabbits of London. The Grand Burrow itself,' she said. 'If this is the way into the palace, and I've discovered it, Papa Ratzi will be sure to reward me!'

'And me!' squeaked Flintskin, doing the Driggle. 'I found it too! I did! I did! I did!'

Mavis joined in and the two Ratzis were so busy celebrating their find that they didn't notice a flash of red fox's tail disappear into a nearby laurel bush.

CHAPTER SEVEN

It was a bright sunny day when Air Force One, the President's jumbo jet, landed at Stansted Airport. Of course, POTUS never travels alone, so the plane was full of people. There was POTUS'S wife, also known as the First Lady (naturally codenamed FLOTUS), their thirteen-year-old son, and hundreds of officials and Secret Service agents from the White House. The President had also brought along his big black car, nicknamed 'the Beast', a shining, armour-plated Cadillac with bulletproof glass and an arsenal of rocket-propelled grenades, night-vision optics, tear-gas cannons and pump-action shotguns all there to keep POTUS safe.

Air Force One came to a halt on the tarmac in front of two welcoming parties. One was the Prime Minister and a large gathering of officials and photographers, the other was ST-BT, lurking in the shadows and reclining languidly on the bumper of the Prime Minister's gleaming Jaguar.

At last the big door of the jumbo jet opened and the President stepped out with his wife and son. They stood together at the top of the steps and waved. At the same time, a large door in the bottom of the plane opened and the luggage began to be unloaded and packed into the waiting cars. Everyone was so busy going about their business that they didn't notice the small hatch of Air Hutch One open at the other end of the plane.

As the cameras clicked and the flashes flashed and POTUS descended the steps, the Rabbits of the United States who had travelled with him hopped on to the tarmac towards their own greeting party headed by Zeno. Like the human Secret Service who protect the President, ROTUS wore dark suits and ties with crisp white shirts. Each rabbit had a pair of dark sunglasses and a special earpiece to make sure they could always be in touch with each other if they needed to spring into action. While humans might carry pistols, ROTUS carried conker guns. The commander shook hands with Zeno, who escorted them all to the Beast.

With a quick movement, a secret hatch was opened in the belly of the car and ROTUS jumped in one by one and in the blink of an eye all thirty were inside. By the time the President had reached the car, the whole troop were strapped into their special seats, ready to travel the final leg of their journey to Buckingham Palace in London. Zeno saluted as the car sped away.

If Shylo had been impressed by the Royal Rabbits of London, he was to be awestruck by the American rabbits.

These were not Hopsters but Jack Rabbits and, just like everything in America, they were somehow super-big and super-glossy. When they entered the great hall in The Grand Burrow, everyone gathered on the floors above to watch. They leaned over the balconies, hundreds of curious faces, to view these large, tough-looking rabbits stride in, sunglasses a-glint and dark suits sharp, conker guns tucked into holsters under their jackets.

Shylo stood beneath the chandelier in the great hall with Clooney, Belle de Paw and Laser and watched with a mixture of excitement and awe. He was very happy that these strapping rabbits were on *their* side.

HOW TO SPOT A ROTUS!

They are American rabbits so they speak with American accents.

The tops of their ears are not pointed like English rabbits, but rounded.

They have very long and powerful hind legs.

They have the newest and most sophisticated gadgets.

They usually wear dark sunglasses, wrap-around style.

When they are not dressed in dark suits, they like to wear baseball caps and bomber jackets – with badges of the American flag sewn on to them.

They like to chew gum.

They always have white earpieces in their ears and little microphones at their mouths to talk to the Commander and each other.

Nelson waited at the far end of the hall to welcome their commander. He did not look excited or awed for he had met many important rabbits in his long life and was not easily impressed.

Zeno grimaced at the eager faces watching from above, jealous that the Americans were getting so much attention. 'Show-offs,' he muttered crossly under his breath, as he escorted two very important-looking Jack Rabbits towards Nelson. One was a big red buck with a scar running down the side of his face, the other was a light brown doe. They both wore dark suits and wrap-around sunglasses and were clearly in charge.

'May I present Special Agent Huntington L. McGuire the Third?' said Zeno so loudly that the chandelier tinkled above them.

'Call me Hunter,' said the Jack Rabbit in a clipped Boston accent, putting out his paw.

'And Special Agent Lola Estrada,' Zeno continued.

'Lola will do,' she said with a grin, shaking Nelson's paw. '*Hola.*'

From his place beneath the chandelier, Shylo nudged Laser. 'Why did she say "oh-la"?' he whispered.

'Because she's from Miami where many people speak Spanish,' Laser replied. Then she grinned. 'In fact, in Miami, even the alligators speak Spanish!'

Nelson nodded solemnly. 'I suppose you're in command, Hunter?'

'No, I am the commander,' replied Lola.

Nelson was impressed. 'Right you are, Lola,' he said. 'Now let me introduce you to our Hopsters.' The Generalissimo waved over Clooney, Belle de Paw, Laser and Shylo. When the Jack Rabbits saw Shylo, they tried hard to hide their surprise, but the small rabbit noticed the looks and it hurt. He lifted his chin and stood as tall as he could and put out his

little paw. Hunter and Lola shook it, almost crushing it with their powerful grip.

'Don't be deceived,' Nelson said to Hunter and Lola with a smile. 'Shylo is the most dangerous of all my rabbits.' The Jacks stared at Shylo with curiosity, wondering how a feeble-looking bunny with an eyepatch could possibly be a danger to anybody, but the old buck didn't appear to be joking.

Laser winked at Shylo. 'Muscles aren't everything, you know,' she said.

Zeno, of course, disagreed and gave a loud click of his tongue.

'Now that you're here, we have work to do,' said Nelson. 'Tomorrow night is the Royal Banquet and we must prepare. Come, let me take you to the war room.'

CHAPTER EIGHT

In the war room, Hunter and Lola were at the map table, discussing the President's schedule with Nelson and Zeno, while Laser was ready to mark the hotspots with her croupier stick. Belle de Paw was spying through the periscopes and her greedy eye had spotted the Queen's dressing table laid out with sparkling rings, bracelets, brooches and tiaras in preparation for the Grand Banquet.

I love mes diamants, she thought, hatching a plot of her own.

Clooney was lounging on the sofa, studying photographs that ST-BT's Backstreet Brushes had just sent over of a couple of Ratzis prowling about the Weeping Willow. Shylo stood awkwardly at the side of the room, longing to be given something to do.

Just then, Frisby, the Major-domo, rapped on the big doors with her ceremonial baton and, in a very fluffily-buffily voice, announced Rappaport.

The blotchy, mangy rabbit shuffled into the room. 'You called, Generalissimo,' he said.

'Ah, Rappaport,' Nelson replied, looking up from the map table. 'Explain to our American allies the problem we are having with the Ratzis.'

Rappaport began to tell them about the threat posed by the rats, but at the mention of those repellent creatures Hunter and Lola looked at each other in alarm.

'We have a problem,' said Lola.

'A *serious* problem,' Hunter echoed.

'I'm listening,' said Nelson in the calm voice of a commander who has seen everything and is impressed by nothing. Shylo felt very confident that, whatever the problem was, Nelson would be able to sort it out.

Lola lowered her voice for she was about to reveal the most confidential state secret. 'The President is terrified of rats,' she said. '*Aterrorizado!* Pet-rif-ied!'

Nelson frowned. The President was tall, muscular and seemingly fearless. It was well known that he had once been in the Marine Corps, the fiercest division of the United States Armed Forces which was made up of some of the bravest people in the world. Nelson was not surprised by much, but he was surprised by *this.*

'Ah,' he said, scratching his chin thoughtfully. 'Well, most people aren't fond of rats'

'No, you don't understand,' Lola interrupted. 'When

the President sees a rat . . .' She paused, afraid to expose such an embarrassing flaw. 'He goes white, his eyes bulge and he trembles all over!'

'When he sees *two* rats,' Hunter added, 'his teeth chatter and his knees knock together.'

'When he sees *three* rats, he loses all control and jumps up and down and screams,' Lola said.

'So what will happen if he sees a *swarm* of rats?' Zeno asked, grinning crookedly.

Lola looked at Hunter. Hunter looked at Lola. They shook their heads. 'We don't wanna even think about it,' they replied in unison.

'This is not good,' said Rappaport, fidgeting anxiously.

There was a long pause. 'So it's up to all of us to make sure the President does not see a rat,' Nelson replied calmly. 'Let's go through his schedule again and see where the dangers lie.'

'Right now, the President is having lunch with the Prime Minister at Number Ten,' said Lola.

'Burgers and pecan pie, his favourites,' added Hunter.

'We have ROTUS following the President's every move,' Lola said.

'Good,' exclaimed the Generalissimo. 'Then what's he doing?' He turned to Laser.

'He's meeting with the American Ambassador at 2.30 p.m., the head of the Bank of England at 3.30 p.m. and Ed Sheeran at 4 p.m.,' she said. 'He's visiting Pinewood Studios at 5 p.m. and meeting the cast of *Eastenders* at 5.30 p.m., then he's having a private tour of Hampton Court Palace at 6 p.m.'

Nelson nodded thoughtfully. 'Good. Then we will cover all those locations alongside our American friends. Lola and Zeno, we need a joint unit of Jacks and Thumpers to go immediately to Number

Ten. I want all exits and entrances covered, do you understand?'

Zeno's fur bristled, which it always did when he was irritated. 'My Thumpers can deal with this,' he said, flexing his muscles to show the Americans how strong and capable he was. 'We don't need the Jacks' help.' He lifted his chin and glared at Lola, who stared back at him arrogantly. Lola didn't like anyone telling her what to do either.

'He's *our* President,' she objected, stepping towards Zeno. 'You should stay here and guard your Royal Family.' Her sharp eyes flashed.

Zeno puffed out his chest in anger, standing his ground in front of Lola.

Nelson looked from one to the other as if he was appraising naughty schoolchildren. 'In order for this State Visit to be a success, we must work *together*,' he said patiently. 'Lola, while your ROTUS are on *our*

territory, they will work with the Royal Rabbits and I will give the orders. Do you understand me?'

'Of course,' Lola replied quickly and stepped back from Zeno.

'And Zeno, Lola and ROTUS will be given the respect they deserve while they are our guests.'

Zeno scowled, but he wasn't going to disobey his leader. 'Understood, Generalissimo,' he said.

'Now go,' Nelson commanded, giving Zeno a warning look as the muscly buck lolloped out with Lola.

Shylo didn't think Zeno was going to enjoy working alongside ROTUS.

Nelson put a paw on Shylo's shoulder. 'While Zeno and Lola take their units to Number Ten, I want *you* to help Belle de Paw at the periscopes. I need to know everyone who comes in and out of the palace and be updated on anything suspicious. Is that understood?'

'Yes, Generalissimo,' Shylo replied, pleased to be

given such an important job.

'Hunter, Laser and Clooney, we should plan your movements at the banquet tomorrow night. I want you in the Banqueting Hall. We must leave nothing to chance. Rappaport, see what else you can glean from the web.'

Shylo was relieved *he* wasn't being sent to the banquet — the thought of coming face to face with those corgis again filled him with terror. He wasn't sure he'd be quite so brave a second time.

CHAPTER NINE

Shylo hopped over to the periscopes.

Belle de Paw was very happy that the little bunkin was going to help her. 'Oh, it is such hard work manning these periscopes all on my own,' she complained, fanning herself with a pad of paper. 'I'm so busy. I only have one pair of eyes and there are dozens of rooms in the palace.'

'Why don't I take half and you take the other half?' Shylo suggested eagerly.

'No, I need a rest. I'm sure you can manage them

all while I take a break. I won't be long.' Before Shylo could object, Belle de Paw had thrust the pad and a pencil into Shylo's paw and flounced out of the room, her silk dress and feather boa floating like a puff of blue smoke behind her.

Shylo was not put off by the long row of periscopes attached to the ceiling, but he was a little daunted by how high up they were: much too high for a small rabbit like him to reach. But Shylo was nothing if not clever. He hopped around the room, collecting big hardback books, and piled them up directly beneath the first periscope. Using the books as a step, he was able to reach it and pull it down to his eye level. Through the glass eyepiece he was able to see the shoes of maids polishing the silver in the pantry. After he had seen what was going on in that room, he wrote down the time and details of the shoes, then moved on to the next. There was **THE THRONE ROOM**,

THE WHITE DRAWING ROOM and **THE MUSIC ROOM**. For every periscope, he had to laboriously move the pile of books.

There was much coming and going in the palace, but the shoes seemed to be either those of maids and ladies-in-waiting, or footmen, butlers and police officers. Shylo had been hoping he'd see the Royal Family. He remembered Belle de Paw telling him that the Queen wore sensible, square-toed shoes, while the King wore shiny black brogues. The Princess of Scotland, their daughter, favoured red-soled stilettos while her younger brother, the Duke of Cumbria, loved biker boots, and his wife, an Indian princess, only wore beautiful Jutti shoes turned up at the toes. But he saw none of those shoes, which was disappointing.

When he got to the periscope with **HER MAJESTY THE QUEEN'S BEDROOM** written on it in big gold letters, he recognized not a pair of shoes but a pair of paws. A pair of fluffy *amber brown* paws! It was Belle de Paw! Shylo gasped as he realized she must have decided to go and steal some more jewels for her collection.

Shylo watched with rising anxiety as those amber paws hopped across the carpet towards the dressing table. He turned the periscope to see the polished court shoes of Lady Araminta Fortescue, the Queen's lady-in-waiting, entering the room. Now he felt sick with worry. He turned the periscope back to Belle de Paw. For a second, he couldn't find her, but after he turned it again, a little to the right, a little to the left, he spotted her blue dress trailing down the legs of the chair in front of the Queen's dressing table. The amber doe was standing on the chair, on tiptoes, leaning over the jewels.

Shylo was aghast. What if she was spotted by Lady Araminta? Belle de Paw was risking her life for

a gem. He turned the periscope again to see the lady-in-waiting's court shoes make their way towards the dressing table. Shylo turned back to Belle de Paw; she had climbed down from the chair and was now peeping out from behind one of the dressing table's legs. The lady-in-waiting's shoes stopped. Shylo jerked the periscope just as four dog paws trotted into view. His heart stalled. The lady-in-waiting reached to pat the dog, Shylo saw her hands swinging into view, but the corgi had already dashed across the carpet to the dressing table. Shylo turned the periscope again, searching for Belle de Paw. She was no longer there.

Shylo knew he should be checking the other rooms as Nelson had instructed, but he couldn't. All he could think of was Belle de Paw, lying in the jaws of a corgi.

Shylo glanced at Nelson. The Generalissimo was still at the map table with Laser, Clooney and Hunter.

The small rabbit longed to tell him what he had seen, but he didn't want to betray Belle de Paw. He knew the Generalissimo would be very angry. Shylo wrung his paws and one of his big ears drooped over his eyepatch.

Just when he was beginning to despair, the big doors opened and in Belle de Paw swept, like a rabbit empress.

She smiled broadly at Shylo. 'I'm sorry I took so long. I fell asleep. What a lovely rest,' she gushed. 'A lovely, lovely rest. I feel like a new rabbit!' Shylo noticed a big sapphire brooch, in the shape of a star, glittering and sparkling on her dress. It hadn't been there before. She saw Shylo looking at it and touched it with her paw. 'This?' she said with a small smile. 'Oh, the Queen will not notice. When you have so many, what is one less?'

At the top of the Shard, the Ratzis waited once again for Papa Ratzi's orders. They had scoured London for information they could use against the President and the Queen, but so far had found nothing of use. They had also tried to find the secret entrances into the palace, but had found none that were not heavily guarded by the Royal Rabbits. They were all very worried that Papa Ratzi would be angry with them.

U haven't found anything to help us ruin the visit? I am disappointed in my Ratzis!

Just then, Slippery Mavis slithered forward. 'I have a plan,' she said, rubbing her glistening paws. The rats held their breath . . .

What is ur plan, Mavis? It had better be good.

'I've found the entrance to The Grand Burrow,' she said and there was a collective gasp of amazement from the seethe of rats behind her.

Well, I am impressed. What do u suggest we do with that information?

'I'm going to create a distraction so that we can kidnap Shylo.'

Very good! Mavis, I put u in command of all operations. If you succeed, u will be greatly rewarded.

Mavis's fur quivered with delight and she glared at Flintskin in case he decided to claim that he had found the secret entrance too. But he just scowled crossly.

'Fellow Ratzis!' she screeched. 'This is what I want you to do . . .'

At dawn the following morning, at Mavis's command, the Ratzis grabbed their Ratzi-blades, which are a little like Rollerblades but much faster. On the sole of each boot was a single row of six big wheels. Not only did these Ratzi-blades make the super-rats even taller, but they gave them astonishing speed. The rats slid their hind paws into the boots and fastened them tightly. They had cameras strapped over their shoulders, rucksacks full of junk food and fizzy drinks on their backs, and smartphones at the ready.

With a whirring of wheels, the Ratzis whizzed towards the exit chutes, jumping into the pipe-like slides one after the other, whooshing in seconds to the secret tunnels that lay in a vast network beneath the

pavements of London. As humans walked, bicycled and drove above them, the Ratzis spread out in their hundreds, blading swiftly through the underground passageways, in the direction of the Weeping Willow.

CHAPTER TEN

Shylo was awoken by a loud babbling. It seemed as if the entire Grand Burrow was shaking with activity. Hurriedly, he threw on his jacket and scampered to the great hall. Rabbits were gathered on every floor, peering over the balustrades, as Zeno assembled his Thumpers in the hall below. The army of rabbits stood to attention in rows, awaiting their orders from the Marshal of the Thumpers. Shylo stood on a high step of the staircase and watched in fascination. He had yet to see the Thumpers in all their glory and

it was very exciting. He could see Hunter deep in conversation with Lola and deduced from their grave expressions that the Jacks were not included in this expedition, whatever it was.

Pricking his ears, Shylo listened to the conversations around him.

'Ratzis are circling the Weeping Willow,' murred one rabbit.

A second muttered, 'This isn't a drill. This is the *real* thing!'

A third, who sounded very knowledgeable, added: 'The Ratzis have discovered our secret entrance, but our Thumpers will see them off.'

As you know, Shylo was a very curious rabbit. It was curiosity that had originally led him to Horatio's burrow on the forbidden side of the forest back home, and it was curiosity that drove him to read newspapers and books, but too much curiosity can sometimes be a dangerous thing.

Now curiosity inspired Shylo to follow Zeno and the Thumpers as they made their way outside to St James's Park. There he saw the Ratzis circling on their Ratzi-blades. A dark, menacing pack of the super-rats, with their oily backs hunched and their teeth bared, were weaving in and out of each other. Shylo stood beneath the tree and watched, wracking his brains as he tried to think of something he could do to help.

From the front of his assembled army, Zeno raised his paw: 'Monsters! Charge!' he shouted and the

Thumpers marched towards them. To Shylo's surprise, the Ratzis began to retreat, quickly swivelling round and skating away into the park. He hadn't expected it to be that easy.

'Halt!' cried Zeno and the Thumpers stopped marching. Zeno punched the air with his paw in jubilation. 'You truly are monsters!' he shouted to his Thumpers. 'Look how quickly the cowardly Ratzis ran away!'

Shylo felt an uneasiness in his belly. The kind of worry that starts at the paws, climbs into the chest and then spreads out until one's whole body is tingling with apprehension. It was the same sort of sickly uneasiness that he used to feel when his siblings played practical jokes on him.

'Zeno!' he cried, suddenly realizing that the rats were simply a diversion. But before he had time to get Zeno's attention something terrible happened.

The whole world was plunged into darkness as a sack was thrown over Shylo's head. He was pushed to the ground then hauled into the air. Panic gripped him. He squirmed, trying to escape, but the opening of the sack had been tied into a firm knot. He felt himself being carried. The bag swung, making him feel sick. He kicked with his hind legs and burrowed with his front paws, but the sack was too thick and after a while he gave up, sitting in a sorry heap at the bottom. The smell of Ratzi invaded his nostrils. He had no doubt as to who his captors were.

Then he heard voices.

'We got him!' croaked a deep Ratzi voice gleefully.

'*I* got him!' came the reply, a female voice this time. '*You* were useless. I'll make sure Papa Ratzi knows exactly how rubbish you were! He'll lop off a little more of your tail. And I'll be famous.'

'Shut up, Mavis! I'm carrying him now, aren't I?'

'Only because I made you, Flintskin, you lazy slob!'

'He's not as light as I thought he'd be.'

'Stop complaining and do your job. We have work to do.'

'Let's take him to the Shard. The Doctor will make him talk and then we'll find out all of the secrets of the Royal Rabbits of London.' Flintskin laughed. 'No one survives the chest press!'

By the time Shylo was released from the sack, he was feeling so sick he could barely move. Gingerly, he crept out to find himself surrounded by Ratzis. *Hundreds* of Ratzis. The smell was so repulsive he could barely breathe. The rats peered at him. What was more alarming than their bulging, greedy eyes was the saliva dribbling from their open mouths. A couple were actually driggling. Shylo was afraid that

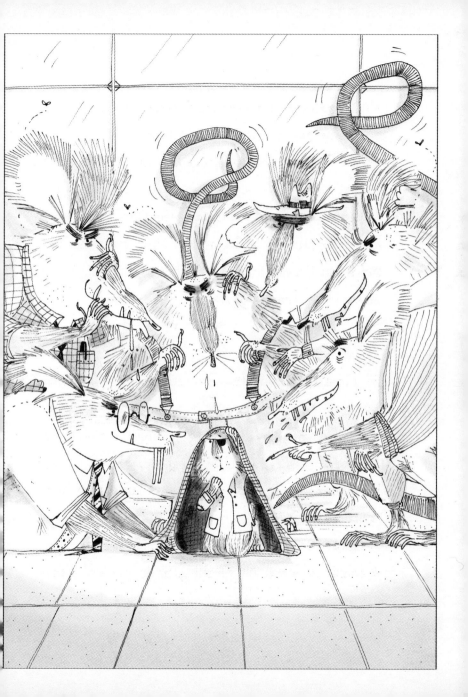

they might *not* interrogate him as he'd overheard, but gobble him up instead.

He trembled with fear. He had begun to believe himself brave, as brave as any of the Royal Rabbits, but he wasn't. He wasn't brave at all. After the triumph of his last adventure, he now felt such a fool because he couldn't even muster a small slice of courage in the face of this many rats. He was terrified.

'Don't be afraid, little bunny,' said one of the fattest Ratzis. 'We're not going to eat you . . . yet!' He guffawed and his greasy belly wobbled. Shylo's ears had fallen over his face and his bottom lip was trembling as he tried to hold back his tears.

'What's that he's got on his eye?' asked a scrawny one.

'What happens if I ping it?' chortled a scruffy one crawling with fleas. He put out a long claw and pulled the elastic like Maximilian, Shylo's brother, used to do. When it snapped back, it gave Shylo a twang of pain. Suddenly, his fear turned to anger and he clenched his paws.

'You do that again and I'll set the corgis on you!' he shouted, surprising himself. 'They made a hearty meal out of those rats I found in the tunnel!' Shylo didn't even come up to the rat's waist, but his outburst had been so furious the rat stepped back in shock and Shylo felt empowered for a brief and blissful moment. But then it was over. Rough claws grabbed him by the shoulders.

'Enough!' Shylo recognized the voice. It was the female rat who had captured him, Mavis. She really was very ugly, Shylo thought, peering up at her misshapen jaw and drool-speckled lips.

Suddenly, the sound of 'Rock-a-bye Baby' silenced the muttering rats. Words appeared in the air

and Shylo read them in astonishment, wondering how they got there.

Well done, Mavis. I am proud of my clever Ratzi. I have been busy too and have discovered something very pleasing from an informer in The Grand Burrow itself.

At the shocking mention of a traitor at the heart of Royal Rabbit Headquarters, Shylo stopped feeling sorry for himself and stared at the words in horror. What rabbit would betray Nelson and why, he wondered?

The President's greatest fear is rats! Isn't that the best news ever! I command u to invade Buckingham Palace at dusk in ur seething hundreds and swarm into the Banqueting Hall. Now u know where the secret entrance to The Grand Burrow

is, u shouldn't have too much trouble fighting ur way in. My Ratzis r far superior to those rabbits! I want to see the President looking like a fool on live TV, broadcast all over the world. America will never recover from the humiliation and the British will be blamed. The world will SHAKE!

The words stopped and the rats looked from one to the other with excitement. They now had a plan and it was a good one. It was the best plan Papa Ratzi had ever had.

'Come, little rabbit, you have an appointment with the Doctor,' said Mavis, anxious to get inside the palace so that *she* would be the one to film the Ratzi-swarm.

'Uh, the Doctor's sick,' said Thigby, scratching his bottom where a flea was burrowing into his fur.

'Sick?' Mavis rounded on the flabby rat. 'What do

you mean he's sick? He's a doctor!'

'He ate a gigantic hamburger and the lettuce in it made him ill,' Thigby explained. 'Serves him right for eating salad. Yuk!'

'Then we'll have to wait until he's better. In the meantime, take this silly bunny to the Gym and guard him,' she commanded and Thigby nodded obediently.

The Ratzis' Gym was positioned at the very tip of the point of the Shard. Everything in it was brand-new. Shiny leather and chrome running machines gleamed like metallic statues, facing an entire wall of glass. But of course not one Ratzi had ever used this room for the purpose of exercise; instead, they treated it like a torture chamber.

Thigby dragged Shylo to the Gym by the scruff of his neck and, as they entered the room, Shylo shivered. The Gym didn't have the same ratty scent as downstairs; instead, the air was thick with the smell of fear. Thigby, who had only one ear, a short nose, swollen cheeks and round, bulging eyes, leered at his prisoner. He was a very sweaty rat — so sweaty that it ran like a stream over his flibbery belly, leaving a trail.

'It's just you and me, bunkin. I could eat you now. I could have you all to myself,' he said, stepping closer and covering Shylo in his stinky, ratty breath.

'But you wouldn't want to upset Mavis,' said Shylo, thinking quickly. 'And what would Papa Ratzi do to you?' Thigby sneered, but backed away, leaving Shylo alone in the room.

The rabbit hopped to the glass wall and gazed out over London. If anyone had looked up at that moment, they would have seen a very small, very frightened rabbit staring out of the enormous window. But Shylo didn't imagine anyone knew where he was. He didn't imagine anyone even knew he'd been kidnapped. He

was all alone, waiting to face the Doctor, whoever he was, and he longed to cuddle his mummy with all his heart.

Shylo started to cry. He'd let everyone down: Nelson, who had believed in him, and Laser, Clooney, Zeno and Belle de Paw who had so readily embraced him into their fold. He didn't deserve their affection. He didn't deserve to be a Royal Rabbit. He didn't deserve his Red Badge or his medal. He now felt foolish for having sent it to his mother. Real Royal Rabbits didn't get kidnapped by Ratzis! He had been stupid to celebrate his success after one triumphant adventure. One lucky escape didn't make him brave or clever. He was a small country bunny with an eyepatch to cure a squint: *that* was the truth. How could he ever have believed he was a Royal Rabbit?

ST-BT was in the Fox Club, sitting at a roulette table, spinning the wheel, when the doors opened and a slight, wiry vixen walked into the room dressed in a scarlet tracksuit. ST-BT raised his eyes and watched her approach. Red Velvet was one of his most valuable spies. She could stalk along drainpipes, dance on rooftops, sashay through railings and at night she padded empty streets as if she ruled the city. She was as swift as the wind and as nimble as an acrobat and there was no creature in the whole of the city to touch her.

ST-BT nodded, inviting her to approach. 'You have news?' he asked.

'The Ratzis have kidnapped Shylo and taken him to the Shard,' she replied.

At this, ST-BT's face darkened. He liked the little rabbit. He might be a feeble-looking creature, but he had shown wit and intelligence and, if Horatio had seen qualities in him worthy of sending him into the heart of the Royal Rabbits, then he must be a very special rabbit indeed. 'Shylo's in mortal danger,' he said, putting down the dice. 'He won't survive the Doctor. No one does. We must inform Nelson at once.'

CHAPTER ELEVEN

Shylo stood for a long while, staring out over the city, wondering what the Royal Rabbits were doing and whether they knew of his capture. He hoped that, if they did, they would not risk their lives trying to rescue him. He wasn't worth it. He couldn't stop thinking about what Papa Ratzi had written, that there was an informant in the very heart of The Grand Burrow. It was unbearable to think that someone had betrayed Nelson and all the noble rabbits who worked so tirelessly to protect the Royal Family.

The time the banquet at Buckingham Palace was due to begin kept drawing ever closer and there was no way for Shylo to warn his friends of the terrible Ratzi plan to humiliate the President on live television. It was dreadful and he felt thoroughly useless. If only he could think of a way to escape.

Shylo hopped helplessly about the Gym, trying to find an exit, but there wasn't even a tiny hole for him to crawl through and, even if he was strong enough to break the glass wall, the only way out was falling hundreds of metres to the ground.

The hours went by and he watched the sun climb over the Thames and hover above the Houses of Parliament. Then he watched it slowly sink in the western sky and he began to be afraid. He had been locked in the Gym all day, but it felt like a week.

Just then, the entire building seemed to vibrate with a whirring, turning sound. Shylo pricked his ears and listened. The door opened and Thigby slunk in.

'It's dusk. My comrades are setting off for the Weeping Willow,' he said gleefully. 'They're going to storm The Grand Burrow!' He jumped up and down with excitement, his floppy belly jumping up and down too as if it had a life of its own. 'They're going to frighten the President and embarrass the Queen and it will all be on live TV!'

Thigby started to driggle. What a gruesome sight that was! Ratzis, like parents, should not be allowed to dance, especially in public. 'By nightfall, there won't be a single rabbit left, and you, little bunkin, will be the cherry on the cake,' he gloated. 'Take your last look at London.'

Shylo stood by the

glass and gazed out over the city. The sun had slid further down the sky, turning the river to gold. It was nearly nightfall and there was nothing Shylo could do to warn the Royal Rabbits. Nothing. He was helpless. He banged the glass with his red-stamped paw.

Back at The Grand Burrow, Nelson and the Hopsters were growing increasingly worried about Shylo. No one had seen him since that morning, when he had watched the Thumpers setting off to fight the Ratzis. Belle de Paw feared he had ventured outside to observe the action and been taken by a bird of prey, but the others were doubtful; Shylo was much too clever for that. It wasn't until ST-BT swished in to see Nelson that the horrible truth was revealed.

'The Ratzis have taken Shylo,' he told the Generalissimo.

'The Ratzis? Are you sure?' he growled. 'Why would they take Shylo?'

'Because he's an easy target and they want information,' ST-BT replied smoothly.

'I thought it was strange that the Ratzis retreated so quickly,' said Zeno, shaking his head. 'They were simply creating a diversion so they could capture Shylo.'

'That little bunkin is much too curious for his own good,' lamented Belle de Paw with a sniff. 'He should have stayed in the safety of The Grand Burrow.'

'We need a plan,' exclaimed Laser.

'And fast!' Clooney added.

The fox shrugged for it was not his problem. 'You should send a rescue party, or that poor little rabbit is done for.' He made for the door, then turned round and added: 'Shame, that small bunkin had a lot of potential.' A moment later, he was gone.

Nelson solemnly gathered everyone together to try to plan Shylo's rescue. But, as they talked through different scenarios, it seemed hopeless; how could they reach Shylo in the Ratzis' lair?

Shylo was doomed.

Just then, Rappaport burst in. 'I've intercepted another text from Papa Ratzi,' he updated them gravely.

'And?' Nelson asked. 'What does it say?'

'They're on their way here.'

'Here?' Nelson banged his baton on the floor. 'Good greengage!'

'They only way into the palace is via our tunnels,' said Rappaport. 'Now they know our secret entrance, they'll be hoping to catch us by surprise and fight their way into the Banqueting Hall. This is a threat such as we've never had before. They must be plotting something diabolical.'

'Then we'll be ready for them!' said Zeno and his booming voice made everyone jump.

'Zeno, mobilize your Thumpers. Lola, call your Secret Service Jacks,' Nelson commanded. 'Remember, we're stronger when we work *together*.'

Zeno glanced at Lola and his fur bristled. Lola looked at Zeno and her eyes smouldered. But this was not the time to be competitive. They had a common enemy to defeat.

'Lola,' said Zeno, standing over the map table. 'Let me show you the tunnels.' He pressed a button and the map of the palace disappeared, and in its place the network of tunnels that ran beneath it appeared in yellow lines and flashing lights.

Lola put her paws on the table and gazed at it with interest. 'Right, I propose we place Secret Service *here* and Thumpers *here*,' she said, pointing at specific places on the map. In spite of the threat, both rabbits were excited at the prospect of battle. It was what they'd been trained for.

'My Thumpers will be the first line of defence when the Ratzis reach the Weeping Willow,' said Zeno.

'And my Jacks will be right behind them,' said Lola.

Zeno looked at Lola and Lola looked at Zeno and then, surprisingly, they both grinned. Aware that they were on the same team now, fighting for the Special Friendship between their two nations, they felt a rousing sense of camaraderie.

'I got your back, Zeno, my friend,' Lola added gravely.

'And we'll be the stronger for it,' said Zeno.

While they planned tactics, Laser was pacing up and down, slicing the air with her whip. 'But what are we gonna do about Shylo?' she asked.

'Shylo won't be able to hold out against their torture. If we don't do something, they'll find out all

our secrets,' said Clooney.

'If they haven't already,' Lola added grimly.

Belle de Paw gasped and her delicate ears drooped. 'No! I have faith in Shylo. I don't believe he will tell them anything! But we have to rescue him.'

'The Shard is like a fortress.' Nelson shook his head regretfully. 'I fear Shylo is lost. The threat to the banquet is more important. We took an oath and we must honour it, whatever the cost. Hunter, Laser and Clooney, I want you in the Banqueting Hall, now. Belle, I need to you to check the periscopes and keep an eye out for any sign of the Ratzis.'

Belle de Paw hopped sadly to the periscopes and pulled down the one inscribed with the name **BANQUETING HALL**. She put her eye to it and saw the shiny shoes of butlers, footmen and maids as they put the final touches to the table in preparation for the dinner. Then her vision misted and a tear trickled down her cheek. She had grown very fond of Shylo in the last few weeks and now it seemed she would never see that floppy-eared bunkin again.

CHAPTER TWELVE

Having caught Shylo, Mavis and Flintskin had celebrated with a feast of junk food they'd found rotting in the park bins before quickly falling asleep. They'd been awoken sharply by the rumpus of all the other rats strapping on their Ratzi-blades and wheeling out of the building. This was their chance to win fame. There was no way these two ambitious rats were going to stay in the Shard when there was a prize to be won for filming the President's humiliation.

Of all the Ratzis, Mavis was the craftiest. She and

Flintskin did not set off, as the others did, towards the Weeping Willow, but towards the palace itself. Mavis knew the Royal Rabbits would be distracted chasing the Ratzis on blades at the Weeping Willow, and she could use that to her advantage and sneak in another way without being seen. The Royal Rabbits would never expect a Ratzi to enter the palace through a door or window.

Mavis decided that she would somehow attach herself to a guest attending the dinner, then she'd be taken directly into the Banqueting Hall itself where she'd have a perfect view of the President and the Queen. Her video camera would be ready for her to film the moment the rats swarmed and be the first with the footage of a terrified President. That would earn her Papa Ratzi's reward and maybe even her own reality show on one of his TV channels. She'd become a star.

She looked across at Flintskin skating beside her as she whizzed down the tunnel on her Ratzi-blades. *Every star needs a sidekick,* she thought.

Back at the entrance to The Grand Burrow, Zeno was busy shouting orders at his Thumpers. His voice was so loud and booming that it echoed off the trees in the park and sent squirrels fleeing into the branches. He formed the elite rabbits into lines beneath the Weeping Willow, ready to face the Ratzis.

Lola assembled ROTUS, dressed in their dark suits and shades, behind the line of Thumpers, as well as sending a select few to hide among the bushes with their conker guns at the ready. The Special Relationship between the United Kingdom and America might have been on the brink of disaster in the human world, but it had never been stronger in the animal world.

'I'm grateful you're here,' said Zeno to Lola as they discussed their final plans.

Lola grinned. 'We're a good team,' she replied. 'We'll blast those rats back to the sewers where they belong.' She put up her paw and Zeno gave it a friendly slap.

'The sewers are too good for them,' he growled.

'After, we'll come back and celebrate our victory over a glass of carrot juice,' Lola added.

'A glass of our *finest* carrot juice,' Zeno corrected. 'Only the best for our American friends!'

Laser, Hunter and Clooney took the small wooden lift that used to be a dumb waiter up into the palace. If the Ratzis managed to break through the lines of Thumpers and Jacks, they'd head straight for the Banqueting Hall. The three rabbits would wait for them there. Laser had her bow and arrows and her

whip, Hunter had a conker gun and Clooney had a hand mirror tucked into his dinner jacket. (You may think that a little vain of Clooney, but remember that shiny surfaces enabled him to secretly observe people.) They all hoped Zeno and Lola would ensure that they didn't have to use their weapons.

The three rabbits crept through the rooms, keeping to the shadows as much as possible to avoid the coming and going of staff as they prepared for the banquet. At last, they reached the Banqueting Hall. Their secret entrance to this room was normally concealed inside a wooden cabinet placed against the wall, but their hearts sank as they realized the cabinet had been moved and a table with a display of flowers had been put there instead. There was no way they were going to get in by their usual method. The big double doors, which were open, would be their only chance, but sitting in front of them was a corgi. This particular dog was called Messalina; she was one of the Queen's favourites and, because she was the fiercest, she was head of the Pack of nine that lived at the palace.

The trio of rabbits dived beneath a chair as a maid hurried past. There were feet everywhere and the corgi looked more alert than ever. Indeed, Messalina's ears were pricked and her nostrils were flaring.

The three rabbits looked at each other. How were they going to get into the Banqueting Hall?

Mavis and Flintskin poked their heads out of a gutter in the pavement on Birdcage Walk, a short skate from Buckingham Palace. They could see lots of people at the palace gates. The guards in their bright scarlet

uniforms and furry bearskins stood to attention like statues outside and shiny black limousines drove slowly into the grounds of the palace, carrying important guests. Mavis skated swiftly along the pavement, keeping to the edge, but she needn't have worried: everyone was much too busy watching the goings-on at the palace to notice the two rats.

To reach the palace, Mavis and Flintskin would have to cross two busy roads and get through the police checkpoint which had been set up to inspect guests' invitations before allowing them inside. But Mavis and Flintskin were not afraid of cars or people. They were not afraid of anything - except the all-powerful Papa Ratzi, and *he* had ordered them to crash the banquet. So crash it they would, and nothing would stop them.

Crossing the first road was not difficult because there was very little traffic. The rats reached the green on the other side and tried to speed across it. But it

wasn't easy to skate on the long grass and Flintskin fell over on his bottom with a yelp.

'Idiot!' muttered Mavis crossly, though she was struggling too. A mole peeped out of the earth, spotted the rats and swiftly dived back into the ground again, muttering through a mouthful of soil: 'Humph! A lot of traffic on my lawn today!'

At last, the Ratzis reached the second road. The palace was in their sights. They waited for the traffic lights to go red, then zoomed across it, disappearing among the hundreds of feet that stood in front of the gates. A poodle on a lead barked at them, but Mavis and Flintskin were skating too fast to be bothered by a pampered dog. They dodged shoes and boots, stilettos and sandals and took refuge against the stone gatepost. They panted with exhaustion and their black hearts raced with the sheer wicked thrill of it all.

'Now what?' Flintskin asked.

'See that limousine?' said Mavis, pointing to one of the many cars moving towards the gates. 'We're going to hold on to the bumper and it'll take us inside. Come on!' she commanded.

They skated beneath the car while the police officer was busy at the window, speaking to the chauffeur. Just as the car began to move on, they sped out and grabbed the back bumper. They were very exposed, but the police officer was now waving forward the next car and the tourists were craning their necks to see who was inside. The only person to notice them was a small child who pointed and shouted, 'Mummy! Rats on skates!'

'What nonsense,' said his mother, who was busy taking photos on her phone. 'Look at the celebrities!' she cried excitedly.

Mavis and Flintskin held on tightly as the car drove

through a large archway into a courtyard, beyond the prying eyes of the tourists.

'Let go!' shouted Mavis, just before the limousine drew to a halt outside the grand entrance where a red carpet had been laid down for the guests. The two rats lifted their paws off the bumper and skated with some difficulty (because gravel is very tough on small wheels) into the shadows beside the wall.

'We made it,' said Flintskin happily, taking off his Ratzi-blades and packing them into his rucksack.

'Yes, we have,' said Mavis, doing the same.

Flintskin looked around and smiled as he spied a drainpipe leading up the side of the building. Rats love nothing more than climbing drainpipes.

'Ladies first,' he said with a smirk.

'Idiot!' said Mavis.

CHAPTER THIRTEEN

Shylo was fed up. He was tired of being stuck high up in the Shard and not being able to warn the Royal Rabbits of the Ratzis' invasion plan. No one was going to rescue him - he knew that all the Royal Rabbits would be busy trying to protect the Queen and the President. He had to escape using his own wits. He remembered what Belle de Paw had said to him after his nightmare: 'If you believe in yourself, there is no limit to what you can do.'

He had let them down by being captured, but he

could make it up by escaping. He just had to *believe* he could do it. He might not be strong or swift but he was clever. He stopped feeling sorry for himself and ran his eyes around the room in search of an idea.

Shylo studied Thigby. He was the most unfit and sweatiest rat Shylo had ever seen. Also he was clearly very stupid. Surely Shylo could use both those two flaws to his advantage.

'What are all these machines for?' he asked innocently.

'Exercise,' Thigby replied.

'This one looks very strange,' said Shylo, putting his paw on the black control panel of the running machine.

'It's called a treadmill. Humans run on it, but it can be dangerous for weak little rabbits.' Thigby grinned gleefully at the delicious thought. 'You'll discover how it works when the Doctor comes.'

Shylo tried not to look frightened; the Doctor sounded very scary. 'How does it work?'

Thigby, who up until this point had never been given an important job in his life, was only too happy to show off his knowledge. 'You stand on this track and this button makes it move.' He pressed the green button. 'You see, the ground is starting to move. Press plus to go faster and minus to go slower. And this red button *here* stops it very fast.' Thigby pressed it and the belt stopped.

Shylo's mind lit up with an idea. It was a brilliant idea. If it worked, it just might be brilliant enough to get him out of here!

'Hmmm,' said Shylo, scratching his chin thoughtfully. 'How fast can you run on it?'

'I might not look very fit, but looks can be deceptive,' said Thigby, wiping his brow. 'I can run very fast actually. Faster than you could even imagine.'

Shylo pretended not to understand. 'But you can't run on this, can you?' he asked.

'Why not?' said Thigby huffily.

'Because, like you said, you don't look very fit.'

'Well, I *am!*' Thigby retorted crossly.

'OK, if you say so,' said Shylo, giving a little chuckle, which annoyed Thigby because it was very obvious that the little rabbit didn't believe him.

'I'll show you how fit I am!' he declared. He jumped on to the belt and pressed the green button. The belt started to move beneath him and he began to walk.

'Walking is easy. You have to run to prove that you're really fit,' said Shylo.

'I know that!' said Thigby. Panting, he pressed the plus button and the belt moved faster.

'That's not very fast. I think that you were lying about being fitter than you look.'

Thigby was really running quite fast now. He pressed

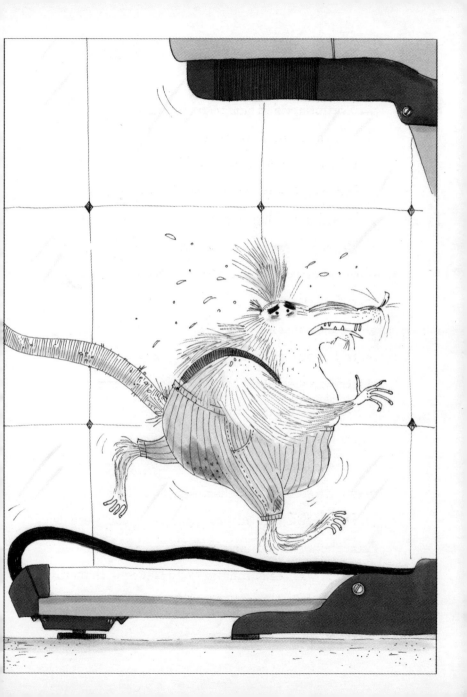

the button again. The speed dial was climbing swiftly and the belt was moving faster.

And faster.

And faster.

'This . . . is . . . a bit . . . too . . . fast,' gasped Thigby, splashing sweat all around him.

'Even for a fit rat like you?' said Shylo.

'Yes, even for me.'

'Would you like me to stop it?' Shylo asked.

'Yeeeeeees!' cried Thigby.

Shylo pressed the red button that Thigby had shown him, making the belt stop with a jolt. Thigby flew off the running machine and into the air. He was catapulted at such speed that he hit the glass wall and, before Shylo had even realized what had happened, Thigby had smashed through the glass, leaving a Ratzi-shaped hole. Shylo stared as the rat hovered in thin air, his stumpy legs still running, hundreds of metres over the City of London.

The fat, flibbery rat fell the seventy-two floors of the Shard with a shrill scream that ended abruptly with a sharp *splat* sound.

'Hmmm!' Shylo thought aloud. 'I guess Thigby was right. Gyms can be extremely dangerous, after all.'

Not wasting another minute, Shylo made a dash for the door, hoping that Thigby hadn't locked it. His luck was in: Thigby had been so sure of his skills as a captor he'd left the door unlocked.

Scurrying out into the corridor, Shylo's heart thumped against his ribcage. How was he going to find his way down? What if he encountered any Ratzis on the way?

The Shard was a maze of shiny corridors and bright rooms containing desks, laptops, studios and screens. There didn't appear to be rats anywhere. Shylo presumed they'd all gone to the palace. He looked around frantically, but he couldn't see an obvious way out. He knew they must have some sort of exit that took them to the ground, but he didn't know where to find it.

Shylo opened doors, peered round corners, even tried to open windows, but with no luck. At last, he found a panel labelled **SHAFT 7** and he opened it and stepped into a dark tower. He hopped on to a large steel surface which seemed to be held up by thick cables. Suddenly, the floor fell away beneath him. It was then, in a rush of panic, that he realized what he was standing on was going down.

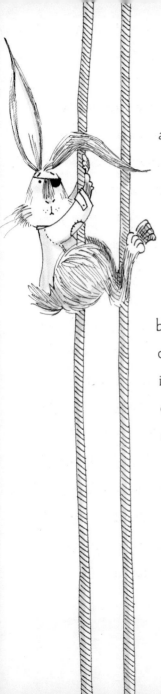

Shylo held on to one of the cables as the 'thing' rapidly descended. It went at such a speed he thought he'd left his ears behind, but no, they were there, sticking straight up in the wind.

It stopped once or twice and Shylo could see through a crack beneath him that, each time it did so, people got in. Eventually, it seemed to reach its final destination at the bottom because everybody got out. Shylo decided to do the same, and hopped off the roof and perched on a ledge, pressing himself against the wall, between more cables. Luckily, he was just small enough not to be squished as the 'thing' refilled with people and then whooshed up again. Had he been a big buck like Zeno he would surely have been crushed. He looked around and found he was at the bottom of a dark tower.

Shylo was afraid. The big metal doors in the wall, which had allowed people into what he presumed was the building, were closed and he didn't know how he was going to get out. He did not want to be there when the 'thing' descended again. Slowly, he clambered into a pit at the very bottom and hopped about, searching for an exit. He found a hole just big enough for him to squeeze through. It smelled of rat, although it was the stench of ordinary, communal-garden, public-drain, rubbish-bag rats, not Ratzis (there's a big difference!) which was a relief.

Shylo hopped gingerly along the tunnel, hoping that it would lead him out. It was silent except for his pounding heart. The earth was damp, but Shylo was used to living underground in the Warren so he didn't mind. Then, to his joy, he saw a shaft of weak light. He quickened his pace. The ratty smell was masked now by the stench of rotting food. He made it to the beam of light and looked up to find that it came from a hole in what seemed to be the bottom of a dustbin. But he couldn't see how to reach the light. He closed his eyes and wished that he was safely back on the farm with his mother. And, just as he was about to give up hope of ever finding his way out, something grabbed him and pulled him swiftly to the surface.

His heart stopped.

He was done for.

It was all going to end here.

His nose twitched. He smelled the once frightening, but now terribly reassuring, taint of fox mixed with butterscotch.

'You didn't think we were going to just leave you

there, did you?' said ST-BT, dusting Shylo down and straightening his eyepatch.

'But how did you know I was going to be here?' Shylo asked, overwhelmed with relief.

'I trusted you'd think of a way of escaping. Neat move with the running machine. Lethal. Ruthless. Sly like a fox. I was watching you with my super-strength, high-powered binoculars. You'd make a good fox if you didn't have funny bunny ears and a tail like a feather duster.'

'How are we getting back?' Shylo didn't think he could do any more running.

ST-BT glanced around warily and lowered his voice. 'Don't tell anyone,' he whispered, 'but I'll make a special exception and carry you on my back.' Shylo looked surprised. ST-BT lifted his nose and assumed a lofty expression. 'I don't normally give rabbits rides. It's not my thing. But we need to get back and fast.

My mole spy near the palace has reported that two Ratzis have broken into the banquet. He spotted them hitching a ride on the back of a limousine. We must hurry.'

'Isn't it a long way?' Shylo asked.

ST-BT grinned raffishly. 'Not for a fox with my kinda SWISH.'

CHAPTER FOURTEEN

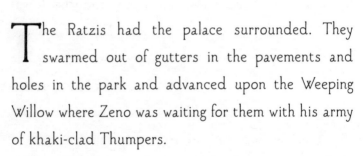

The Ratzis had the palace surrounded. They swarmed out of gutters in the pavements and holes in the park and advanced upon the Weeping Willow where Zeno was waiting for them with his army of khaki-clad Thumpers.

The sight of the Ratzis' ambush was a terrifying one, even for Zeno who was a very brave rabbit. They were whizzing about on Ratzi-blades, weaving in and out of each other, their narrow eyes glinting like razors as they assessed the enemy. With cameras slung over their shoulders, rucksacks on their backs and smartphones in their pockets to remind them of Papa's instructions, the super-rats looked more dangerous than ever.

This time they didn't flee. This time there was no little rabbit to kidnap. This time they were intent on invading The Grand Burrow itself, which would give them access to Buckingham Palace, and the Royal Family and the President inside it. This attack was bigger than anything they had ever done before, but Papa Ratzi had demanded it and they'd do anything for their boss.

The Ratzis stopped skating.

A terrible silence descended on the park.

Zeno, at the head of his Thumper army, put up his paw.

The Ratzis arranged themselves in a tight formation. For a long moment, no one moved. Then with a mighty

shriek they whizzed towards the Thumpers.

Zeno dropped his paw. 'Charge!'

In Buckingham Palace, Clooney, Laser and Hunter watched helplessly as Messalina sat guarding the double doors to the dining room. The other corgis of the Pack had now joined her: Agrippina, Helmsley, Lucrezia, Lady Macbeth, Livia, Imelda, Moll and Jezebel. Slowly, the guests began to appear. The Royal Family mingled with the assembled guests, women in long dresses and diamonds and men in tailcoats and white bow ties. If Clooney had been a little bigger, he would have blended in beautifully in his tailcoat and scarlet bow tie.

'What do we do?' Laser hissed.

'We're trapped,' said Hunter. The three rabbits looked about them. There were shoes everywhere. The guests were making their way into the dining room and Messalina and the Pack did not look likely to move.

'There's nothing we *can* do,' said Laser. She glanced at Clooney hopefully. 'Now would be a good time to come up with a plan,' she added.

'*You're* meant to be the brains, Laser,' said Clooney with a grin. 'I'm just the beauty.'

'I don't see anything funny about this, Clooney,' Laser snapped. 'Shylo has been kidnapped, Zeno and Lola are fighting the Ratzi army outside, and we can't even get into the Banqueting Hall. We can't let Nelson down. We can't let the President down and we can't let the Queen down.' Laser and Clooney bowed their ears.

'Gotta love ya,' muttered Hunter, amused by the quaint tradition of bowing ears. 'This royal thing of yours is so charming!'

'OK,' said Clooney, after gazing at himself in his

pocket mirror, which often inspired a useful thought. 'I have a plan. But I warn you, it's not a very good one.'

'I don't care,' said Laser. 'It's the only one we got.'

'Have you read the story of the Gingerbread Man?' ST-BT asked Shylo as the little rabbit climbed on to his back.

'Yes,' Shylo replied, for he had read many stories and that one was a family favourite.

'What happens to the Gingerbread Man when he climbs on to the fox's back?'

'The fox asks him to climb higher so that the river they're crossing won't get him wet.'

'And then what happens?' ST-BT asked smugly.

'He encourages the Gingerbread Man to climb on to his nose, which he does.'

'And then he eats him,' ST-BT said, finishing the

story for him.

Shylo's ears drooped as he was suddenly gripped by fear.

But ST-BT chuckled. 'Which means you're a very brave rabbit climbing on to the back of a fox.'

Shylo's ears straightened with relief. He remembered what Clooney had told him about the Rabbit Rules of Secret Craft. 'I trust you,' he said, settling on to ST-BT's shoulders, hoping that he was right.

'Quite right too,' ST-BT said, loping off, fleet of paw. 'Hold on tight. It's going to be a very swish ride.'

Beneath the Weeping Willow in St James's Park, the battle was raging. There were squeals and screeches, squawks and squeaks as the Ratzis dug their teeth into rabbit flesh and the rabbits plunged their claws into Ratzi flibber.

Zeno, an impressive sight with his bulging muscles and rich black fur, knocked out Ratzi after Ratzi with powerful swipes of his fist. They dropped about him like ninepins, landing on their fat bottoms with their skates above their heads. For a wonderful moment, it looked as if the rabbits were winning, but then the Ratzis used their most potent weapon. They lifted their tails and the farts gusted out with moist abandon, the thunderous sound of them shaking the air which was almost hazy with stinky green mist. They were so strong that Zeno complained that chemical warfare was against the rules.

The big, brave bucks coughed and choked and grabbed their throats.

Was this the end for Zeno's Thumpers?

ST-BT kept to the shadows. Oh, how light those

paws were! He waltzed up pavements, tap-danced along bridges, leaped over roads and foxtrotted across parks until he finally reached the high walls surrounding Buckingham Palace. As Shylo slid off his back, ST-BT wasn't even panting. He looked as if he'd taken a short stroll round the park. Shylo, on the other hand, was exhausted. It had taken all his strength not to fall off. His arms ached and his legs burned and he was gasping for air.

'Follow me,' said the fox, disappearing behind a dustbin. Shylo hesitated a moment, but then the loud siren of a police car made him jump into action and he followed the fox and found that behind the dustbin was a small chute in the wall. He dived through it, coming up on the other side in the garden of Buckingham Palace. ST-BT shook himself and was totally swish again.

It was dark now, but for the golden lights of the

city, which made the sky above them glow orange. Shylo followed ST-BT round a lake and over the lawn to the back of the palace. The fox stopped beneath a sturdy plane tree.

'But how are we going to get inside?' Shylo asked.

'*We* are not doing anything - *you* are,' said ST-BT in his commanding voice. This reminded Shylo of the time Horatio had told him that he was going to have to find his way to London and to The Grand Burrow, all on his own, and his heart suddenly ached for his old friend.

'I'll create a diversion and, when someone comes to see what's going on, you will hop inside,' ST-BT continued. 'Do you understand?' Shylo nodded. 'Good. Nelson will never forgive me if I fail to get you any further than the palace lawn. Now go.'

Shylo darted over the dewy grass and up the stone steps to the French doors. He ducked low and waited.

ST-BT opened his mouth wide and began to make the most extraordinary noise. Have you ever heard a fox bark? It sounds something like a baby crying, a cat screeching and a dog coughing, all in one. Shylo was familiar with foxes, having grown up in the woods, but even he had never heard any of them making a noise like ST-BT.

Suddenly, the door opened and a pair of shiny black shoes stepped out. Shylo didn't wait to see to whom they belonged. He hopped inside and darted for cover beneath a table.

'A fox!' gasped the footman. He gaped in astonishment at the animal that was standing on the grass, staring back at him with a steady, fearless gaze. 'How impertinent!' the footman muttered. Then the fox began to walk towards him with a menacing expression on his face, waving his bushy tail most arrogantly, and the footman hurried inside and closed the door. 'Better make a call to Pest Control,' he said.

ST-BT smiled with satisfaction. Humans really were very feeble creatures. Even Prime Ministers. Without *him*, they could never run the country.

ST-BT glanced at the enormous gold watch on his wrist. It was just after eight o'clock.

Just time for a Butterscotch on the Rocks at the Fox Club before he had to escort the Prime Minister safely home from the banquet.

CHAPTER FIFTEEN

While the rest of the Ratzis were busy in the park fighting Thumpers, Mavis and Flintskin made their way into Buckingham Palace via a small square window in the roof which had been left ajar.

Once inside the palace, they slithered along a corridor, down a narrow flight of stairs and on into the heart of the Royal Family's home. Slithering came naturally to Ratzis.

It wasn't hard to find the Banqueting Hall because of the din - humans make a lot of noise when they're talking. And tonight there were over one hundred of them all chatting at once as they looked for their places at the long tables arranged in a U shape, and waited for the King and Queen and the President and First Lady to enter.

But it was not as easy to break into the room as Mavis and Flintskin had hoped. Messalina and her fearsome pack were still guarding the big double doors.

The two rats watched as the dogs stared at an upside-down waste-paper bin, which was slowly moving across the crimson carpet as if by magic.

'What's that?' hissed Flintskin to Mavis as they hid behind a giant pedestal upon which was placed a marble bust of Queen Victoria.

'It's a waste-paper bin, you idiot!' Slippery Mavis replied.

'But why's it moving?'

'Because something inside it is making it move.'

'Is it one of us? If another Ratzi has sneaked in ahead of us, I'm going to be *very* angry,' he grumbled.

'Oh, shut up,' Mavis snapped. 'It's not a Ratzi. It's a rabbit. Look, you can see the paws.'

Indeed, the waste-paper bin lifted off the ground for a moment and a pair of rabbit's paws was revealed.

'How are we going to get into the Banqueting Hall?' asked Flintskin, scratching an itch on his bottom. 'You think you're so clever, Mavis, but look! We're stuck! We'll never get to film the President now.'

Mavis's narrow eyes darted up and down the corridor and finally settled on a door at the end which kept opening and closing as women in long dresses and jewellery went in and out. **LADIES' ROOM** it read.

'Follow me,' she hissed. 'And be quick!'

Inside the Ladies' Room, an elderly woman, the dour Duchess of Goldborough, who had a neck like a vulture and eyes like buttons, was sitting at a dressing table, applying lipstick very badly in front of a mirror (somehow she had just managed to poke the lipstick into her nostril by mistake which was not a good look), while a much younger woman, an American film star, wearing a multicoloured minidress, was taking a selfie. The Duchess's handbag, which resembled a leather box and was practically big enough to feed a horse out of, was lying open beside her as she tried to get the lipstick out of her nose.

Now that they were inside, Mavis didn't bother to explain her plan to Flintskin. *After all,* she thought, *how much better would it be if I was the only rat to make it into the Banqueting Hall?* With a triumphant grin, she scampered up the curtain behind the dressing table and slipped unnoticed into the Duchess's handbag.

It was filthy: there was even an old tuna sandwich at the bottom. Mavis felt right at home and took a bite.

Flintskin was furious. He floundered in the shadows, not knowing what to do. He scowled and his slick fur bristled crossly as the Duchess gave up trying to get the lipstick out of her nostril with the words: 'If I do it, *everyone* will want to do it.' And she picked up her handbag (with Mavis peeking jubilantly out of it) and left the room.

The American film star was busy posting her selfie on the internet, but she had her large (and very sparkly) crown-shaped handbag tucked tightly under her arm.

Just when Flintskin was about to abandon all hope, he noticed a pair of black court shoes visible beneath the lavatory door. Between the shoes was a green flowery handbag. Flintskin's scowl turned into a smirk. *I'll show Mavis!* he thought as he scuttled

beneath the door and slithered into the handbag. There wasn't much room among the phone, keys and powder compact, and Flintskin was so squished that he was unable to pull in his tail; it hung limply out of the bag in a streak of pink. The lavatory flushed and the woman (who was, in fact, the Queen's lady-in-waiting, Lady Araminta Fortescue) pulled up her knickers, straightened her dress and grabbed her handbag without noticing Flintskin's tail. Nor, as she made her way to the Banqueting Hall, did she notice that the handbag had mysteriously grown heavier. She was much too busy making sure that all the guests had found their chairs.

'Did you see that?' whispered Hunter urgently to Clooney, who was watching Laser inside the waste-paper bin cautiously edging her way across the carpet. 'There was a rat's tail hanging out of that woman's bag!'

Clooney turned to him in panic. 'A rat's tail! Are you sure? Perhaps it's a new fashion accessory!'

'Rats' tails will never be in fashion,' snarled Hunter. 'We have to hurry. If any Ratzis make it into the Banqueting Hall and the President sees them . . .' But it was much too awful to speak about and he stopped. 'We cannot allow that to happen.'

Messalina was now pricking her ears at the strange waste-paper bin. She stood up and wagged her tail. She could smell rabbit. In fact, she could smell rat too. Perhaps there was a rat in there as well as a rabbit. She licked her chops and went over for a sniff. The Pack trotted after her, their lips curled and growling. Inside the bin, Laser tried to summon up all the strength she had. She had a job to do and she wasn't about to let the Royal Rabbits down.

Just as Clooney had planned, with Messalina and the Pack distracted, he and Hunter darted across the corridor, sprinting behind the dogs as they sniffed their way towards the bin, and scurried through the double doors.

Spotting baskets of bread rolls on a sideboard, the two rabbits jumped on to a chair and from the chair on to the table, and dived into the baskets to hide. Gradually, they advanced up the sideboard, leaping from bread basket to bread basket. The Indonesian ambassador told the Duke of Cumbria that he thought he'd seen a rabbit jump out of the bread.

'Unlikely,' said the Duke, wondering if the ambassador wasn't perhaps a little overexcited.

CHAPTER SIXTEEN

Shylo hurried through the palace towards the smell of human beings. His sharp nose picked up the scent easily and he scampered over the crimson carpets, following the smell as it got stronger and stronger. He could also detect dogs, but was in too much of a rush to worry about them. He had to get to the Banqueting Hall and warn the Royal Rabbits of the Ratzis' plan.

In the Banqueting Hall, the Master of Ceremonies brought down his gavel and shouted: 'All stand for

Their Majesties the King and Queen and the President and First Lady of the United States of America!'

The guests stood and turned to face a pair of mirrored double doors situated at the opposite end of the room to the corgis and the sideboard where Clooney and Hunter were currently hiding among the bread rolls. (Clooney was watching the action from the reflection in his hand mirror, which he had poked out of the basket.) An air of excited anticipation filled the room.

Behind those doors, coming down a long red corridor and moving very slowly (at a stately pace), the King and Queen led the President and the First Lady towards the Banqueting Hall.

Beneath the Weeping Willow, Zeno looked across at Lola, who was waiting with her Secret Service Jacks

in the bushes for him to give her the signal. Zeno, outnumbered by the vast seepage of farting rats, now gave it with a nod.

Lola saluted to Zeno and turned to her Jacks and said: '*Adelante, conejos!*' which means 'Advance, rabbits!' in Spanish.

There was only one thing for it: conker guns. As the green mist acted like a poisonous gas and the Thumpers staggered dizzily, a wall of dark suits and big sunglasses moved through it in a long line, then stopped. The Ratzis put down their tails and stared at the unfamiliar Jack Rabbits. Then they saw the guns. They knew very well what they were.

The big Jacks aimed.

'Fire!' Lola commanded.

In the Ladies' Room at Buckingham Palace, the

American film star heard the distant sound of the Master of Ceremonies' voice. She realized to her horror that she was going to be late for the dinner (it is very rude to arrive *after* the Royal Family). In a panic, she tottered hurriedly into the corridor, unsteady on her dangerously high stilettos. As she stumbled towards the Banqueting Hall, she thrust her phone into her crown-shaped handbag, leaving it open in her haste, just as Shylo came bounding round the corner.

Shylo heard the crack of the gavel and the voices quieten in the Banqueting Hall.

He only had seconds to spare . . .

The corgis sat round an upturned waste-paper bin in front of the big doors, ready to pounce. How on earth could he get past them?

Then the open bag swinging in the hands of the actress caught his eye. This was his chance.

Shylo, who by now was very tired of running, mustered one final burst of energy and landed softly in the bag, ears peeking out of the crown.

As the little rabbit rode the bag into the Banqueting Hall, the film star tottered right past the Duchess of Goldborough and Lady Araminta Fortescue.

Mavis poked her head out of the Duchess's handbag and stared at Shylo in amazement.

Flintskin, who was peeping out of Lady Araminta's, gasped in disbelief.

Shylo grinned and saluted.

Both Ratzis were so shocked and furious that their eyes nearly popped out of their sockets.

Shylo would have been triumphant had he not felt so sick. The swinging bag was beginning to make him nauseous. What was he to do now?

CHAPTER SEVENTEEN

The important guests took their places at the head of the table. The President was placed on the right of the Queen, the First Lady next to the King. The gavel hammered again.

Silence.

'Your Majesties, Mr and Mrs President, Your Royal Highnesses, Lords, Ladies and gentlemen, dinner is served!' the Master of Ceremonies cried.

Flintskin popped his head out of the handbag and slunk on to the table. Mavis slipped to the floor and

positioned herself with her smartphone to film the moment the President saw him.

Every eye in the room was on the Royals at the head of the table. Except for the President's.

His were on Flintskin.

He froze. Then his skin paled. His eyes bulged and he began to tremble all over, which was definitely not befitting an ex-member of the Marine Corps. He was about to let out an almighty scream that was definitely not befitting a Commander-in-Chief.

Shylo spotted Flintskin crawling along the table and knew he had to do something and fast. He swung back and forth, back and forth, making the bag move like a trapeze artist in a circus. (Luckily, the film star was so busy staring at the King and Queen that she didn't notice the little bunny in her handbag.) Then, on the third swing, just as the bag reached its highest point, Shylo strained every muscle in his hind legs and sprang out. He didn't think he could do it - he'd never had to jump so high. But one can always do more than one thinks.

With a giant leap, which would have astonished his brothers and sisters back home, Shylo crashed straight into a butler carrying a tray of oysters. The oysters were propelled into the air and rained down upon the guests, sending Flintskin dashing for cover underneath the table.

One particularly heavy shell hit the Duchess of Goldborough right on her lipsticked nostril. As she lifted her hand to retrieve the flying mollusc, she knocked over her wine glass, which toppled on to the spoon in the sauce boat, which, in turn, spun into flight, twisting like a silvery boomerang. A butler reached to catch it, but missed and, instead, knocked into a footman carrying an enormous lobster on a tray. Just as the President opened his mouth to scream, the lobster was catapulted across the room.

Making the most of the diversion, Clooney leaped out and flung himself on to Mavis, sending her smartphone tumbling across the floor, while Hunter aimed his gun from the bread basket and fired a conker at Flintskin. The conker missed by a millimetre and the two rats pounced on Clooney with a squeal.

Shylo landed on the carpet with a soft *poof,* but no one was watching him. Instead, all eyes were on the lobster which was flying through the air in the direction of the Queen.

The President had seen it too and narrowed his eyes as it soared closer to Her Majesty.

Luckily, the President was a brilliant sportsman: able with a racquet, deft with a ball and a superb golfer.

He was also a very chivalrous man: immediately, he forgot all about the rat, shut his mouth and diverted his attention to the lobster. Reaching out quickly with his hand, he caught it, just before it hit Her Majesty right on the nose.

There was a long silence.

Everyone held their breath.

The President stared at the lobster in surprise. Then he looked at the place where the rat had been and saw that it had disappeared.

The Queen turned to him and said: 'Very well caught, Mr President.' Then she sat down and put her napkin on her lap as if nothing had happened.

The room erupted into applause. A footman quickly took the lobster from the President who then sat down, a little shakily, because he really thought he *had* seen a rat and also because he realized he had very nearly screamed in terror in front of the

Queen, a room full of important people and on live television. His wife patted him gently on the hand.

With dinner service now resumed as normal, a footman lifted a bread basket from the sideboard and offered it to the Duchess of Goldborough. Her pudgy, bejewelled fingers settled on a very soft, warm roll. 'Goodness, the bread must be straight out of the oven,' she said, impressed. Just as she was about to take it, the roll twitched and she withdrew her fingers with a gasp. 'I think I'll take *this* one,' she said, picking a cold roll from the top instead.

Messalina and the Pack of corgis were distracted by the excited noise in the Banqueting Hall and, when they looked back, Laser had escaped. However, the dogs were now much more interested in the goings-on in the hall. They trotted in just as the clapping was dying down.

There, under the table, were two big, pudgy rats fighting a rabbit in a tuxedo.

The corgis wasted no time in racing towards them, tails wagging, teeth bared, snarling and growling.

Clooney saw the dogs before the Ratzis did and leaped beneath a chair. Hunter seized his chance as the footman was distracted by the dogs and dived out of the bread basket. The two rabbits shot from the room as fast as their legs could carry them as the corgis chased the rats beneath the table.

This time the dogs did not catch the rats; after all, Mavis and Flintskin were Papa's crack Ratzis. They managed to dart from under the table and shimmy up the backs of the curtains at the end of the Banqueting Hall. Spotting an open window, they dived through it, soaring into the air and landing on the roof of a catering van that was slowly beginning to make its way

out of the palace grounds. By the time they realized where they were, the van was heading down the Mall.

The two Ratzis lay on their backs and looked up at the stars. There are moments in the great adventure of life when it's OK, even well deserved, to fart, and this was one of them. And so they did, happy to be alive.

'Idiot!' said Mavis to Flintskin. 'It's all *your* fault!'

'I thought I saw a small creature out of the corner of my eye,' said the President to the Queen, a little shaken. 'What were your dogs chasing?'

'We don't have small creatures in the palace, Mr President,' said the Queen. 'The dogs were just having jolly good fun chasing each other.' She bent down and lifted Messalina on to her lap and stroked her soft head.

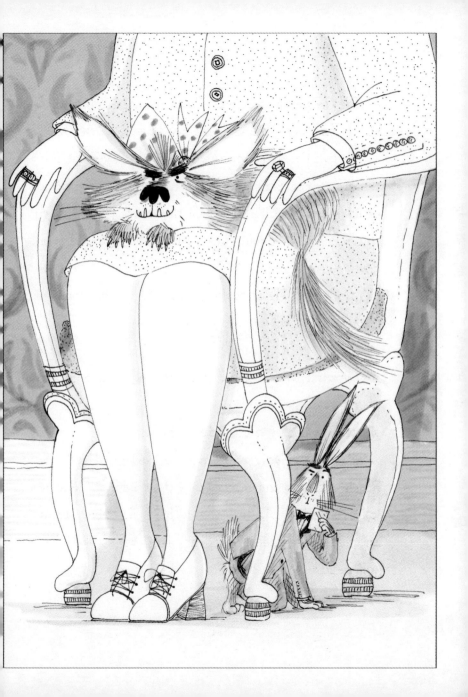

The President frowned. He must have been mistaken.

Outside, the other Ratzis were retreating quickly. Knowing they were beaten, they skated as fast as they could, knocking into each other and clambering over each other in their desperation to flee. They disappeared the way they had come, in a great, greasy river of fur and tails, into the underground tunnels beneath London, and on to the Shard, where they would discover, to their bitter disappointment, that the bunny who was going to spill all the secrets of the Royal Rabbits of London had escaped.

The Doctor, on the other hand, had recovered and eagerly awaited their return.

'That was great,' Zeno cheered, putting up his paw

for Lola to high-five. 'You and your Jack Rabbits are MONSTERS!'

'And your Thumpers were awesome.' Lola slapped Zeno's paw. 'We did it together! I think it's time for a glass of your *finest* carrot juice, don't you?'

Deep beneath the Banqueting Hall, Belle de Paw was watching the drama going on through the periscopes and reporting to Nelson. 'The disaster has been avoided,' she announced happily. 'Shylo's alive and he saved the day!'

'How did he do it?' Nelson asked.

Belle de Paw laughed. 'By being a very brave bunkin!'

CHAPTER EIGHTEEN

In The Grand Burrow, there was more carrot juice than anyone could drink. The Royal Rabbits of London and the Rabbits of the United States had won a tremendous victory and they celebrated with laughter, celery and a lot of thumping of hind paws so that the ground beneath them vibrated.

The battle had not been easy, so there were many injured rabbits, but they joined in the fun, even with their wounds bandaged.

After the feast, there was dancing. Zeno was the

most enthusiastic dancer and he grabbed Lola and pulled her on to the dance floor. Lola showed off her salsa moves while Zeno swung her around and threw her into the air. Belle de Paw took Hunter by the paw and wiggled to the rhythm, and Laser grinned at Clooney, who put out his arm so that he could escort her on to the dance floor too.

Shylo watched with pleasure. The battle had brought the American Jacks and the Royal Rabbits together, and now music took its place and unified them as only music can. He began to sway to the beat and tap his hind paw on the ground. Then someone touched his shoulder. He looked up. It was Nelson.

'You did well, Shylo,' the Generalissimo said, and Shylo's chest expanded with happiness. 'You are the first rabbit to enter the Shard *and* the first rabbit to escape. Tomorrow I want a briefing.'

And tomorrow Shylo would tell him about the

informer in their burrow who had told Papa Ratzi about the President's fear of rats. However, now was not the moment for they were celebrating their success.

Nelson looked down at the little bunkin and frowned. 'Shylo, you should be dancing,' he said, and he was right. Shylo should have been dancing.

But Shylo had no one to dance with. Once again, he felt like an Outsider rather than a Royal Rabbit who belonged. No one seemed to notice him at all.

Then Belle de Paw was standing in front of him. She bent down and smiled. 'Will you dance with me, Shylo? I can see you tapping your paw. I bet you're a wonderful dancer.'

She offered him her paw.

Shylo took it.

Belle de Paw allowed him to guide her to a spot beneath the grand but rather dusty chandelier. Shylo let the music take him. It started as a fizzy feeling in his hind paws, then became a bubbly feeling in his belly and finally grew into a dizzy sensation in his head. His body moved, his arms waved, his legs kicked and his tail wiggled. Belle de Paw stared at him with her eyes wide, clapping her paws and laughing that tinkling laugh of hers that sounded just like sunshine felt. She was certainly impressed.

Because it turned out that this small, skinny and slightly awkward bunny was not just braver than he knew but, just as Belle de Paw had guessed, a good dancer too.

A *very* good dancer.

Fancy that!

EPILOGUE

That night, in a pretty suburban house in a small town in America — California to be precise — there came a soft rustling sound from the sitting room. Outside it was dark and quiet. The humans in the house were asleep.

They imagined their pet rat, whom they had named Nibbles, would also be asleep in his cage. He had been rescued a few years before from a laboratory where unspeakable things had happened to him. These days he lived most comfortably in a big, sumptuous

cage, because the humans who had adopted him felt sorry for how he'd been treated. He was fed special food and spoiled in every way a family can spoil a beloved pet.

Now he got up from his soft sawdust bed.

Nibbles didn't look like any rat you've ever seen. He had a very skinny body and an oversized head. His pink, shrivelled skin could be seen through a thin covering of white fur and his eyes were a cloudy purple. His tail was long, moist and pink and he had claws that looked more like fingers than paws. Yet his face was almost angelic - the curl of a smile on his lips, an upturned, ski-jump snout and sweet, opaque eyes that were large and winning. Adorable!

But there was nothing adorable about this rat.

He climbed the bars of his cage and flicked open the lock with ease. He was much cleverer than a normal rat, cleverer than most humans in fact, and his mind throbbed with terrible visions and brilliant schemes to rule the world. He scampered out and made for the table where the family kept their computer. He had no trouble jumping on to the table and opening up the laptop. Then his long, finger-like claws began to type.

U have disappointed me. I think Mavis and Flintskin need an appointment with the Doctor first thing tomorrow morning.

Papa Ratzi sighed and turned off the laptop. He was not finished with his plans to cause havoc in the world, and neither was he finished with his plans for a weak but troublesome little bunny called Shylo.

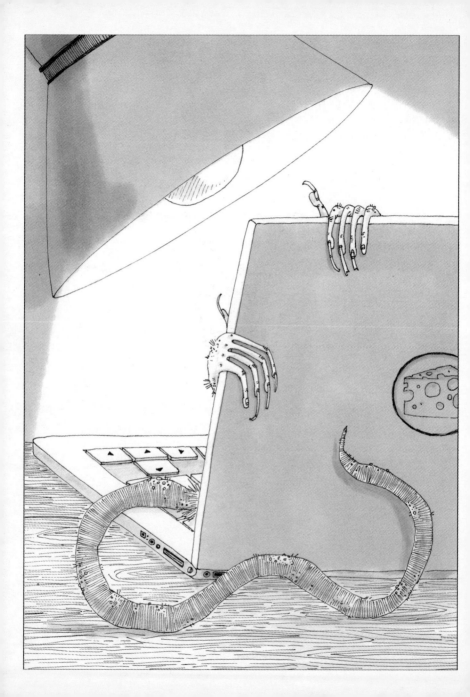

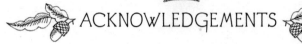 ACKNOWLEDGEMENTS

With our deepest thanks to Jane Griffiths, Kate Hindley, Jenny Richards, Sheila Crowley and Georgina Capel.

Hop over the
page for
some
Royal
Rabbits
extras!

TOP TEN FACTS ABOUT THE US PRESIDENTAND THE WHITE HOUSE

1. The President of the United States is the head of state and the head of government so is a cross between our Queen and our Prime Minister. They are elected by the people and make the rules of the country.

2. The President travels to other countries to meet with heads of foreign governments and works out agreements concerning trade.

3. The President is also the Commander in Chief of the United States Armed Forces and can send them anywhere in the world to protect the country's interests.

4. The President lives in the White House, in Washington D.C.

5. The White House is an office, as well as a home, and every US president has lived there since it was built in 1800.

6. The first President of the United States, George Washington, supervised the building of the White House, but he did not get to live there! It was the second US President, John Adams, who first lived in the White House.

7. The White House has 132 rooms, 35 bathrooms, and is set over 6 levels, to accommodate everyone who lives and works there. There are also 412 doors, 147 windows, 28 fire places, 8 staircases and 3 elevators.

8. The White House also has tennis courts, a jogging track, indoor and outdoor swimming pools, a cinema, a games room with ping pong tables and a putting green. Barack Obama added removable basketball hoops to the tennis court so he could practise his own favourite sport.

9. The White House receives over 6,000 visitors each day.

10. It takes 2,591 litres of paint to cover the outside of the White House - that's enough to fill an Olympic-sized swimming pool!

QUIZ:
Which Royal Rabbit
are you?

1. How would your friends describe you?

a) Brave and clever

b) Kind and beautiful

c) Well-dressed and watchful

d) Loud and muscly

2. What is your favourite food?

a) Celery

b) Caviar, darling!

c) Canapes at a fancy party

d) A muscle-building drink

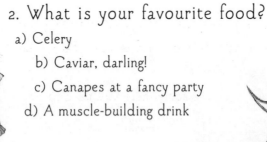

3. How do you like to relax?
a) Reading a book
b) Surrounding yourself with shiny,
   pretty things
c) Dressing up smartly and going out
d) Relax? What's that?

4. What's your favourite thing to wear?
a) Anything you feel relaxed in
b) Something that matches your DIAMONDS
c) A tuxedo
d) Sports wear

5. What would be your ideal job?
a) Something exciting that will take you on
   adventures!
b) Working somewhere you have to be
   glamorous and gorgeous
c) A secret agent
d) Bossing people around

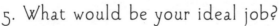

Mostly As
Just like Shylo, people might think you're shy and quiet, but you long for adventure and you're brave, clever and loyal.

Mostly Bs
Just like Belle de Paw, you love glamour and excitement, and you're good at spotting things that other people don't notice.

Mostly Cs
Just like Clooney, you're clever and charming and take pride in your appearance. You always cool and calm, makes you an excellent spy!

Mostly Ds
Just like Zeno, you're strong and brave and you have lots of energy! Sometimes people find you a little bit scary, but you're kind too, so they don't need to worry too much.

BUTTERSCOTCH ON THE ROCKS!

You Will Need:
A bottle of butterscotch syrup
Milk
4-5 ice cubes
Your favourite drinking cup or glass
Cocktail umbrella/straw for decoration

1. Place ice cubes into glass
2. Carefully pour over a small measurement of butterscotch syrup
3. On top of that, add enough milk to just cover the ice cubes
4. Finish with the cocktail decorations
5. Sit back and enjoy!

London Landmarks

The Royal Rabbits love travelling around London
and taking in the sights.
How well do you know London? Do you know what
amous landmarks these clues are describing?

Clue Number One:

This famous landmark can be found
in the Clock Tower at the Palace
of Westminster

Clue Number Two:

Perfect for sightseers, this landmark is on the
banks of the River Thames and takes 30 minutes
to complete a revolution.

Clue Number Three:

Over the years, this landmark has been used as a royal residence, a prison, the treasury, the Royal Mint, a records office, and as a house for the Crown Jewels.

Clue Number Four:

The official residence of the UK's sovereign since 1837.

Clue Number Five:

You can find the Whispering Gallery here and it was designed by Sir Christopher Wren.

Have you read
Shylo's first adventure?

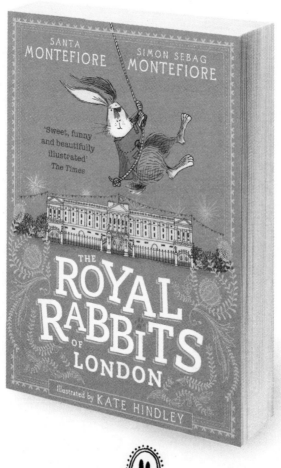

THE ROYAL RABBITS

OF LONDON

will be back!
Look out for a new
adventure coming
Autumn 2018!